ALAN COLE IS NOT A COWARD

ALAN COLE IS NOT A COWARD

ERIC BELL

KATHERINE TEGEN BOOKS
An Imprint of HarperCollins Publishers

Katherine Tegen Books is an imprint of HarperCollins Publishers.

Alan Cole Is Not a Coward
Copyright © 2017 by Eric Bell
All rights reserved. Printed in the United States of America.
No part of this book may be used or reproduced in any manner whatsoever
without written permission except in the case of brief quotations embodied
in critical articles and reviews. For information address HarperCollins
Children's Books, a division of HarperCollins Publishers, 195 Broadway,
New York, NY 10007.
www.harpercollinschildrens.com
Library of Congress Control Number: 2016053557
ISBN 978-0-06-256704-8
Typography by Aurora Parlagreco
HB 03.27.2023
❖
First paperback edition, 2018

*To my mother, Mimi,
who knew I was not a coward from day one
and who never let me think otherwise*

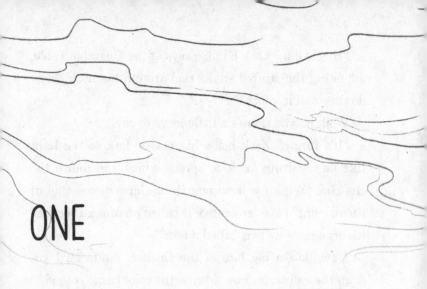

ONE

A guy's life can basically be summed up by two things: how much Silly Putty he's eaten and who made him eat it. There are charts and diagrams to calculate your Level of Wussdom based on whether you ate Silly Putty, say, because you were lazy and you didn't feel like walking to the fridge to get an apple or something, or because your older brother tackled you to the floor and force-fed you leathery, glumpy globs.

Let's just say my older brother's introduced my stomach to so many varieties of random objects, my Wussdom Level is literally off the charts.

On my tombstone they'll carve *Here Lies Alan Cole. Ate a Metric Ton of Silly Putty. His Poop Was Spongy and Could Stick to Walls.* What else is there to even say after that?

"Hey, Alan," Zack Kimble says at the Unstable Table, adjusting the stuffed snake tied around his neck, "why do they call it a fork?"

Well, maybe there's a little more to say.

"It's funny." Zack holds his plastic fork to the light like he's waiting for it to sprout wings and dance the cha-cha. "You know how some things have names that fit them, right? Like, an orange is called an orange because it's orange. Why is it called a fork?"

I swallow a big bite of the chicken sandwich I got from the cafeteria line. "Maybe the color came second."

"The color fork?" Zack asks.

"The color orange. Maybe the color orange is called orange because it's named after the fruit."

Zack slowly lowers his fork. "Wow," he whispers.

That should keep him quiet for a few minutes.

Anyway, sure, there's a little more to say. That in between all the Silly Putty, and the Elmer's glue, and the glitter—which doesn't really taste like much, but man does it tickle going down—

"If you want my honest opinion," Madison Wilson Truman pipes up next to me, interrupting my thoughts again, "a fork is called a fork because it's forked between the points. Haven't you ever heard of forks in the road? Those are different paths branching off from the same point. That's where the term comes from."

Zack looks down at the plastic fork. "I never knew that. I've been using forks my whole life! I'll never eat the same way agai—" He snaps his head to the left and swivels his neck as he looks up at the ceiling; his spiky hair, jutting out at all angles like an electrocuted porcupine, sways back and forth. "I thought I saw a dragon."

Madison gives a little bow in his seat. "If you wouldn't mind 'forking' over a tutoring fee, that would be greatly appreciated." He adjusts the collar of his polo shirt and chuckles, and he actually makes air quotes when he says *forking*.

Zack rummages around in his pocket. "Is thirty-five cents okay?"

Madison frowns.

This is basically life at the Unstable Table, aka the lunch table with a piece of cardboard shoved underneath the one uneven leg. I've sat with Zack and Madison every day since the start of seventh grade at Evergreen Middle School, but we're not friends or anything. I mean, Zack's friendly (like a puppy that isn't housebroken) and enthusiastic (like a flying squirrel who got into the Pixy Stix). And Madison's smart (like a senile owl) and helpful (like a husky with an awful sense of direction). But I operate under a strict no-friends policy. I've had friends before, and they were my friends until my brother got through with them, and then they needed to join support groups for LEGO-related traumas. Not happening again.

Speaking of my brother, there was always this hope with Nathan that maybe someday I wouldn't have to drink my Coke hanging upside down from his arms. Maybe someday I wouldn't wake up to a drawer full of tighty-whities with cottage cheese smeared inside.

That day hasn't come yet. (My lucky underwear was spared, at least.) But he's been quiet since school started, so maybe it's on the horizon. Until that day's officially here, I do the Alan Cole Special everywhere: keep my head low and huddle into my sketchbook, where Nathan can't find me. Someday soon a big, bold cretpoj is going to burst from my fingers in an explosion of paints and colored pencils and even Elmer's glue and glitter, because true artists feed on inspiration wherever they can. A cretpoj, in case you were wondering, is—

"Are you okay, Alan?" Zack asks. "You're quieter than normal."

I want to ask Zack how he can even tell, since I'm always quiet, and since we don't ever hang out or talk apart from having lunch and ASPEN (Accelerated School Placement Enrichment and Nourishment) classes together. None of us even went to the same elementary school. But having a normal conversation with Zack is hopeless. Maybe he'll get distracted by some gum under his seat or something.

Madison gives me a sympathetic look. "Middle school can be a challenging time for anyone, let alone a Sapling. Of course Alan would have a lot to think about."

Evergreen likes to call seventh graders "Saplings," eighth graders "Sprouts," and ninth graders "Shrubs." If you live in a place called Petal Fields, Pennsylvania, in the heart of a place called Flower County (under an hour from Philadelphia!), where the main claim to fame is our enormous and clogged school district, what else are you going to talk about besides plants? My brother is a Shrub and I'm a Sapling. Don't let the terms throw you off—Nathan's no houseplant.

"Like when all those kids asked if you had a girl's name?" Zack asks Madison.

Madison scowls. "Yes. Just like that."

"Or when Jenny Cowper made fun of your weight? That wasn't very funny."

"No," Madison says through a clenched jaw, "it wasn't."

"Oh, or how about when Mrs. Ront kept calling on you about prepositions, and you kept getting them mixed up with conjunctions, and Talia MacDonald had to give the right answer, and she listed, like, twenty-five of them, and all you could come up with was 'because,' and then Mrs. Ront got all screechy and said that wasn't even close to a preposition—"

"I think we get it," I say.

It's obvious to me Zack is asking because he's curious, and he's not trying to be mean, but Madison's face still turns pale. "Honestly," he huffs, "do you ever—"

"There it is!" Zack points at the ceiling and half rises from his seat. "Oh, wait. That's not a dragon. That's one of the sprinklers." He pretends to feed a forkful of corn to the snake around his neck, humming a song as he goes.

Madison grumbles and runs a hand through his buzz cut.

A cretpoj, in case you were wondering, is the term I came up with for my art projects, because one, it's a lot more important-sounding than "project," and two, it's way more fun to say. I'm trying to paint a portrait of a person's face. I can draw trees just fine and I can sketch the best bowl of wax fruit this side of Produce Pitstop, but I've never been able to paint a face. According to Mrs. Colton, faces are "trending" in the art world. Now, if I made a list of things I'm not, "trendy" would come right after "a twenty-foot-tall elephant," but she made me realize that in my favorite paintings, it's the people's faces that keep me coming back—even those weird Picasso ones where their noses are jutting out of their eye sockets. I want to make something that keeps people coming back. I want to make something that's going to change the world.

So that's my goal. And my brother can't take that from me.

Loud laughter from the next table over cuts into my thoughts: Connor Garcia is flashing his trademark big smile at his table of jocks. I bury my face in my chicken sandwich to hide my blush. Without thinking, I take my napkin and dab at my hair, still damp from the morning's swimming class. Then I realize, oh my God, I'm wiping my hair with a *napkin*, and I shove it in my lunch bag.

Connor Garcia would never even look over at the Unstable Table. He'd never come over here with his big smile and sit with somebody like me and act like it isn't weird that somebody like me would ever want to ask somebody like him to the movies or something. Sure, he likes me, but he doesn't *like* me. It's bad enough that being . . . you-know-what is treated like the middle-school version of the bubonic plague, where somehow news of me having a . . . you-know-what on Connor would spread like lice in a kindergarten class, and soon everyone would be . . . I-don't-think-I-have-to-tell-you-what, and the universe would basically explode.

Yet another reason I have a no-friends policy: even friends can't keep secrets.

"Hey, Alan," Zack says. "Do you think I should've worn the sock monkey instead?"

* * *

Leaving the cafeteria is a nightmare at Evergreen. All the seventh graders—I refuse to call myself a Sapling—have lunch together, so imagine trying to fight this unending tidal wave of around two hundred and fifty bodies while the loudspeaker blares some static-y message about fund-raisers or lawn mowers or something—I can't even hear it over the full, spine-shattering loudness of my classmates—and when I think I find a safe place to catch my breath, an arm reaches out and tugs me into an empty classroom, practically dislocating my shoulder in the process.

"Hey, Al," Nathan says.

For the record? It's Alan. I *hate* being called Al. Nathan knows this. Why do you think he does it? (Also for the record? It's Nathan, not Nate. I learned that the hard way.)

The empty, dim classroom makes Nathan's shadow loom larger. Even though I'm almost as tall as him thanks to a last-minute summer growth spurt, it sure doesn't feel that way. "Hi," I mumble.

"Y'know," Nathan says, crossing his arms. "I was thinking." Thinking is Nathan's specialty. Last year he thought about the best way to superglue my hair to the kitchen table. "It's been a while since we've had a good talk. I wanted to invite you to a meeting. Top secret."

"Sorry, I'm busy," I say.

Nathan smiles. "Tonight at ten. On the patio. Come alone. I'll bring the orange juice. We're going to have a grand old time."

The skin on my back starts to prickle. "You really don't have to. I'm sure you're busy. You've probably got lots of other things to do."

His smile gets wider. "You crack me up, Al. Don't be late." He winks at me and walks out of the room.

A secret meeting . . . maybe he's calling a truce. Maybe he's throwing in the towel and giving up his old ways.

Or maybe they'll change my tombstone to *Make That Two Metric Tons of Silly Putty*.

Some people say grace before dinner. They thank family, friends, food, everything in the universe for their meal. At 16 Werther Street, in Petal Fields, Pennsylvania, you don't say anything before dinner. Or during dinner. Or after. You don't say much of anything unless you're spoken to first, and then you say as little as possible. Nobody gets thanked here.

Surrounded by the smells of garlic, tomatoes, and basil, Dad sits at the head of the table. He eats his pasta like he eats everything: deliberately. Nathan, sitting across from me, shoves his food down his throat so fast it probably leaves sparks in his esophagus. You'd think the sooner he gets done, the closer he is to leaving the table, but nobody gets up until Dad's finished. House rules. Mom eats slowly, even though she's normally the first to finish eating.

When Dad eats, he only leaves crumbs on himself and the area immediately around his plate. Tonight, Nathan isn't so lucky, and three minutes and twenty seconds into mealtime a bit of his fettuccine falls onto the kitchen tiles.

Dad freezes midbite, fork hovering near his mouth. Nathan scrambles to pick up the offending piece of food and leaves it on the edge of his plate. He eats a lot slower after that.

I catch all this as I look at my reflection in the plate, staring back at the almost-teenager in the glass. Above the stove, Dad's ancient wooden clock ticks away, older than me and Nathan, maybe even older than both of us put together.

Finally, after he's wiped his mouth and taken a large gulp of water, Dad speaks. "This weekend is the company dinner."

"Can't I stay at Marcellus's on Saturday?" Nathan whines. "He just got a new game and I've got to play it. Al can go instead."

"Your brother the mapmaker," Dad says. "Finally

putting that art stuff to good use. Take some notes, Nathan."

My chest feels a little lighter. Just yesterday Dad praised me for getting a really nice comment from Miss Richter, my social studies teacher, on an essay I wrote with a map I spent a lot of time drawing. Dad normally hates my paintings, but he likes anything that makes us look good.

Nathan scowls at me. He hasn't gotten much praise from Dad since the school year started. The curriculum is probably a lot tougher in ninth grade than seventh. "But Dad, both of us don't need to be there."

"Of course you do," Dad says. "I'm up for a promotion. If Mr. Harrison sees our family together, behaving *perfectly*, I've got a chance of finally moving up in the company. Mr. Harrison's a family man."

"Your dad's right," Mom says. "This is important for all of us."

Dad's been going on about this company dinner for three months. He's been at his job for years, but they've never held a company dinner before this. Every night we talk about it, and every night he grills us on things. Tonight's no exception. "Donald Turner's going to be at the dinner with his family," Dad continues. "His daughter speaks three languages."

"Oh yeah?" Nathan perks up. "*Scio quattuor linguas.* That's Latin for 'I know four languages.' Right, Dad?"

"Mmm," Dad hums. Mom smiles. Nathan looks at me and smirks.

(English, Klingon, Elvish, and Pig Latin, if you were curious. No, actual Latin is not one of them.)

Dad nods. "Is your good dress ready?" he asks Mom.

Mom stops smiling. "Oh, I got caught up with the girls from church. I'll pick it up tomorrow."

Dad frowns, but doesn't say anything. Mom looks down at her plate.

He turns to me. "What sports do you play?"

I don't play any sports. I'm about as athletic as a bag of bricks, and I probably weigh less too. I can't even swim, which makes this year's aquatics program lots of fun. Nathan can't swim either, but the program—and Evergreen's pool—is new this year, so he never had to learn. Something he's definitely reminded me about a few times. But I know what I've been rehearsing to say. "I run long distance, I play shortstop, and I'd show you my motorcycle kick if I'd remembered to bring my soccer ball."

I can feel Dad staring at me. "Uh, bicycle kick," I stammer. "I'd show you my bicycle kick."

"This is the most important dinner of the year," Dad says again. Then, like a hawk clutching its prey, he says,

"Don't disappoint me, goldfish."

I lower my burning red face. Dad only trots out the nickname for special occasions. Nobody cares about goldfish. People don't keep them as pets; they keep them as background decorations. Goldfish are to other fish what ants are to people, except goldfish can't do anything cool like lift ten times their weight. To Dad, I am a goldfish.

As Mom clears the plates, the old clock ticks and tocks, and 16 Werther Street is quiet again.

Let me tell you about my cretpoj.

My cretpoj, in case you were wondering, is going to be the most breathtaking, jaw-dropping, eye-bulging, heart-racing, face-punching piece of art ever created by human hands.

I bet you're really interested now. Well, this is probably a minor issue, but it doesn't exist yet. At all. I don't know who to paint. I've been looking at famous faces—Batman, Mario, a zombie. I even tried the Mona Lisa, because, hey, start at the top, right?

Nope. Not happening. It needs to be of somebody special. But who?

Changing the world is a lot more difficult than I thought.

I won't give up though. Know why?

Tonight, it's the beginning of October, and like the

beginning of every October in Petal Fields, the big sugar maple at the side of my window sways in the breeze to this really nice rhythm only it seems to know. I've tried to capture that rhythm a bunch of times inside my sketchbook ("capture movement" was the assignment I set for myself over the summer). Nathan doesn't have a two-story-tall Muppet-shaped tree rocking back and forth outside *his* window.

I look at Big Green. It's still here. It'll be naked in a few months, and then it'll come back with a new coat. It shines, then fades, then shines again. It survives.

Between the Silly Putty, and the cottage cheese, and the superglue, and the hawks, I'm still here. I haven't given up. I've survived. I'll survive long enough to make my cretpoj.

Maybe *that's* all you need to know about me.

Alan Cole: He Survived.

Well, I guess they wouldn't put that on my tombstone, for obvious reasons.

Of course, right when you think things are pretty good, right when you're about to get going with the greatest artistic effort of all time, right when you're enjoying your majestic green coat of leaves, winter comes.

Because it's 9:58. Show time.

Somehow I don't think I'm going to get asked to show off my motorcycle kick.

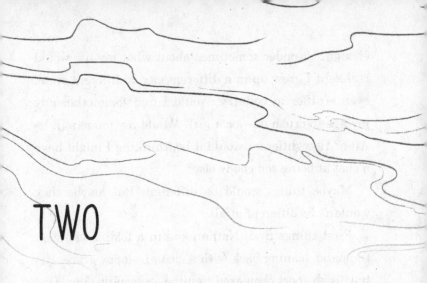

TWO

The house is mostly dark. Mom and Dad go to bed before ten, like all old people, so I follow the patio light streaming in from the backyard. I tiptoe down the stairs, hot lava threatening to bubble up out of my chest. I don't want any part of what Nathan's planning, but he doesn't normally give two roast beef sandwiches about what I want, so I make my way to the patio anyway.

16 Werther Street is nestled in a nice suburban neighborhood, with a little creek running along the back end. The backyard has tall fences and a perfectly kept, pristine green lawn Dad makes sure to tend to every weekend in case the neighbors fly over with a helicopter. The smell of fall hits me as soon as I step outside: moist grass, the neighbors' apple cobbler, air so crisp and clear you could see straight to Seattle if you squinted hard

enough. I wonder sometimes about what my life would be like if I grew up in a different city, a different state, even a different country. Would I find some other guy my age to crush on—or a girl? Would my name still be Alan? How different would it be, thinking I might have a shot at being somebody else?

Maybe things would be different. But maybe they wouldn't be different at all.

First things first: Nathan sits in a folding chair on the patio, leaning back with a casual, sloppy grace. His hair is so short compared to mine, especially since Dad made him cut off the ponytail he'd been growing, which was *not* a happy day at this house, let me tell you. His pajama-clad legs are propped up on the outside table, and next to his bare feet is a carton of orange juice, two glasses from the kitchen, and a piece of paper with three large, loopy letters on top.

Oh crap.

"No," I say.

"No what?" he asks. "You don't even know why I summoned you, young page."

"I know why. I'm not doing this again. You promised."

He holds up a hand. "I promised no more unless I had a good reason. Don't you remember? I always keep my promises."

The lava starts to sink down, deeper into my stomach. "Nathan . . ."

He gestures to the other empty patio chair. Slowly, my feet thudding along like twenty-pound weights, I walk over and slump down.

"This," Nathan says, "is a game of CvC."

I groan.

"Knock it off, goldfish," Nathan says. He slides his legs off the table and the chair clatters on the concrete.

That heat hits my face again. "Don't call me that."

Nathan laughs his hyena's laugh, crackly and full-bodied. "I've got fun things planned for us, Al. Way more fun than we've ever had before."

My hand slowly reaches for the piece of paper in the middle of the table, but Nathan snatches it up first. "Not so fast! You'll want to hear about the stakes first."

"Stakes? Nathan, I—"

"Hmm?" Nathan lifts his head up. "Are you giving me lip, little brother?"

I squeeze my hands tight. The low hum of the cicadas vibrates up my spine.

Nathan takes a sip of his glass of juice. "Let me explain how CvC works. In case you forgot. I mean, you almost forgot I'm your big brother, and I could leave you tied up on the roof all night, and nobody would find you until morning. I hear it's supposed to rain tonight. Poor little Al, all tied up with nobody to come rescue him."

"I know how CvC works," I grumble.

Nathan smirks. "Then why don't you ever win?"

There are a million reasons why I don't ever win CvC, short for Cole versus Cole. In CvC, Nathan gives me a list of things to do, and I give him a list of things to do, and whoever does the most by the time limit wins. Sounds easy enough.

Well, it's not. The tasks Nathan gives me are *impossible*. Well, not literally, but they're impossible for someone like me.

Climb the tallest tree on the block. I've got the upper body strength of a sheet of plastic wrap.

Sing as loud as you can in the cafeteria for three minutes. The game plan behind "Alan Cole: He Survived" does not include drawing attention to myself, especially as someone who has the vocal quality of a vacuum cleaner.

Moon everyone on your bus. Do I need to explain this one?

But Nathan found ways to make me participate, normally revolving around threatening my sketchbook. I climbed Big Green and got stuck up there for hours. I sang obnoxious pop music in the Pine Garden Elementary cafeteria for thirty-two seconds, until a teacher came over and made me stop, and after that Rudy Brighton called me "Aretha Frankole," and it stuck for three weeks.

I'll let you use your imagination on the last one. (Here's a hint: I held up a picture of a certain object in our solar system. Cheating? Well, what would *you* have done?)

Even after doing all that, Nathan still won, because he always shot down or changed everything I suggested until he was left with the easiest junk he could complete in an hour—but not before he got to have all the "fun," of course. Even when I'd complete a few tasks, Nathan never worried, because he could do everything in twenty minutes and win.

I want to say all that, but I'd rather not find out how far down Werther Street I can see from the roof, so I stay quiet.

Nathan stands up and joins his hands behind his back. "Don't look so sad, young squire. There are stakes now, so it isn't just for our personal amusement any-more—now there's things we can *win*. And, of course, things we can *lose*."

"Why are you doing this?" I ask. "If you want something from me, take it. That's how it's always been anyway."

Nathan stops smiling. "Because I'm punishing you, of course." This is the usual refrain: I've done something wrong, and Nathan has to be the hero and set things right. Even though I've learned to stop asking what horrible sin I've committed, I still feel like I deserve it. Like he's Batman and I'm the bank robber, about to get a batarang in the rotator cuff. This probably comes from my earliest memory, lying in bed sick as a dog after leaving the window open painting my first sunset. Dad kept screaming, "Everything is your fault!" I don't even know what I did wrong. It's a big leap going from getting yourself sick to causing the apocalypse. But some things just stick with you, you know?

"Plus," Nathan keeps going, "I could use a break from studying. I need something fun in my life. I get a nice reward if I win too. You'll help me out, won't you?"

I look at myself reflected in the glass on the table. "Nathan, come on."

"Oh, I'm sorry," Nathan says, now with bite to his voice. "Is Miss Richter's favorite student too good to play with his big brother?"

I can't help it. I snort. "Is that what you're punishing me for? Dad doesn't even—"

In a split second Nathan is looming over my chair, dark eyes hidden by shadows. He growls, "I've been busting my butt in ninth grade for a whole month and I've gotten nothing, and all you have to do is draw maps, or get high scores on easy math tests, or remember to tie your shoes, and all of a sudden everyone holds a parade in your honor. What do I get? Nothing. Must be nice. You make me sick, goldfish."

"Um," I mumble, the lava bubbling a little. "What if I say I won't play?"

Now Nathan laughs, in control again. He laughs so loud I swear Dad and Mom must hear him. Of course, Dad sleeps on the opposite end of the house, and snores, and only punishes us (yes, both of us) if he catches the act. As for Mom, Nathan says she used to discipline us back when we were little—even though I don't remember it—but now Dad makes those calls. Along with pretty much all the other calls.

"Al," Nathan says, "you don't have a choice."

A sudden voice in my head yells, *Hey, Aretha Frankole, sing us another song!* "Sure I do," I say, feeling particularly brave.

"Oh yeah?" Nathan asks.

"S-Sure I do," I repeat, feeling considerably less brave.

Nathan holds up a hand. "You don't get it. You have to play. That's part of the stakes. If you don't play, a very bad thing will happen to you."

I don't get it. I give him a blank stare, like a stupid goldfish.

"So," Nathan says, the corners of his mouth twitching. "Who is he?"

The lava almost shoots out of my throat. "W-What?"

"Y'know," Nathan says. "Your little crush. Who is he?"

The words get stuck. Even the noises get stuck.

Nathan rests his hands on the back of his chair. "Poor, poor Al. You've really got to get into the habit of deleting your search history. 'How to tell if you are gay.' 'What to do if you have a crush on another guy.' I mean, really?"

"I lock my computer," I squeak.

"'The0ldGuitarist.' Your password's the name of that Picasso poster you have hanging in your room, with a zero as the *O*. I don't know what Miss Richter sees in someone as stupid as you. If you want to be a worthy opponent, young apprentice, you can start by having something to really fight for. So. Who is he?"

I wonder if it's possible to have a heart attack at the age of twelve. "I was looking it up for a friend," the goldfish says, clamming up.

"Oh yeah?" Nathan asks. "Who?"

I don't say anything. I can't throw anyone else under the bus, plus Nathan knows I don't have any friends. (And he should know, because he's the reason why.) Trying again. "I'm not g-g-g-g—" I try to breathe. No luck. "I'm not like that."

"Yeah, right," Nathan says. "What about that time we went into Abercrombie and Fitch and you stopped walking and stared at that model for five minutes? What about Jonah, the pastor's son? You always watch him in church with your mouth open and your eyes glazed over, like you want him to give you a big ol' kiss. Isn't that what you want, Al? To kiss the pastor's son?"

"No," I say, my breath hitching in my throat, my face turning full-on fiery red, my shirt stained with sweat. "No, it's—it's not—I'm not—"

Nathan slowly walks over to my chair. "But it's not Jonah, is it? It's someone at school. That's who you're in loooooove with. You're going to tell me who it is. We can do this the easy way, or we can do it the fun way. What's it going to be?"

This is the worst-case scenario. Like, the absolute worst-case scenario. The president of the United States could knock on my door with a news crew and say, "Alan Cole, you've been chosen to live under the earth's surface for the rest of your life with the Mole People," and it wouldn't be as bad.

Here are my options: I can keep quiet and not tell Nathan anything, but he'll beat it out of me anyway. I could give up the info from the start, but then he'll know, and, ugh, why is it turning out this way? When did everything go from "kind of okay" to "worst possible thing to happen in all of recorded human history"?

He takes a step forward and the goldfish swims across

the backyard as fast as his little fins can carry him.

But didn't I tell you I don't know how to swim?

Nathan tackles me in seconds. I try crawling out from under him, but he grabs the back of my head and forces it down into the grass, rubbing it into the dirt. When he's done with that, he pulls my hair back, making me yelp, spins me around, and pounds me with punches in my stomach and chest over and over again, until I'm dizzy and bruised. When he's done with that, he digs his elbow right into my gut, almost making the lava inside spill out.

When he's done with *that*, he parts my bangs and strokes my cheek.

"Poor Al," he says. "You make me do this. You have to go and act like you're special. So who is he? I can go all night."

As Nathan pins me to the grass, I think of a third option. "Vic Valentino," I spit out.

Nathan considers this. Eventually, he nods. "Was that so hard?"

He gets off me. I sit up, amazed my plan worked. Nobody at Evergreen Middle School is named Vic Valentino (at least I hope not). Nathan would never imagine me being clever enough to use a fake name. But now what?

"So here's the stakes," he continues, pacing around

our darkened backyard. "Play the game, and I won't tell anyone about your thing for lil' Vickie. But if you ditch on me, I'll make sure all of Evergreen knows, and then it won't just be me who wants to rub your face in the dirt. And I don't even want to think about what Mom and Dad'll do. We got a deal?"

Oh God, Mom and Dad. The second I started middle school, Mom started asking me about girls, and Dad practically insisted I need to get a girlfriend by the end of the seventh grade so I don't "end up like Nathan," who's gone up until ninth grade without any girls interested in him. They're almost pinning all their hopes for grandkids on me. I'm not sure being . . . you-know-what is even in their vocabulary (apart from being an occasional slur). "What's stopping you from telling everyone after you win anyway?" I try not to whimper as I rub my stomach and wipe the grime from my cheeks.

"What, my word isn't good enough?" Nathan reaches down and tugs a clump of grass off the ground. "I always keep my promises. I knew you'd want a little more security though, so how about this: I set off the stink bomb in the Evergreen teachers' lounge last year."

My eyes get wide. "That was you? I heard they couldn't use the lounge for a whole week!"

"That was me," he says. "Marcellus dared me. When you go up to your room, you'll even have evidence I did it. Now you know my secret. If I try to cheat or change the rules or tell your secret without you giving me a reason to, you can tell mine. I won't tell yours as long as you cooperate, so you need to do the same. You keep me in line, I keep you in line. No loopholes. Understand?"

I nod, even though the twisted logic is zigzagging around my head so fast I can barely keep it straight. The important thing: Nathan says he won't tell anyone if I play along. Got that part at least.

"Now," Nathan continues, pacing faster. "If I win this game—and let's face it, my track record is pretty good—you're out. If you know what I mean."

I rush to my feet. "You can't do that!"

"Of course I can." He rests his hands on our shed. "I will, if you lose. When you lose. Then everyone will hate you. Instead . . . instead of me." He rubs the back of his head. "Hey, I don't care if you're gay or straight or whatever. It's not my problem. But I'll still tell the world if it makes them all hate you."

I almost say, *they wouldn't all hate me.* Zack and Madison *probably* wouldn't, just because they don't have anyone else to talk to, but I can't picture anyone else who wouldn't. Even Connor. But . . . "There's got to be something else you want," I say. "Something else I can give up if you win."

Nathan sneers. "Already trying to weasel your way out, huh, Al? I don't want anything else from you. I just want to watch you squirm."

"But—"

"Walk away from the game, and it's the same result. Pick your poison."

I look down at the grass as a light breeze rolls through my hair.

"In the unlikely event *you* win," Nathan continues, "you may ask of me one favor."

"Gee," I grumble, "you're really going out of your way there."

"What do you mean? One favor is a pretty big deal. The possibilities are endless! Of course, the favor can't involve anything that would put my life or well-being at risk, and it definitely can't involve being nice to you."

Nathan turns around and lunges at me from the shed. When I flinch, he laughs, then waves at the outside table, where the paper sits. "There are seven tasks for you to complete by next Friday morning. They're all things you *could* do by the time limit, but they're not going to be easy for you."

Like I'm looking at the brochure for my own funeral (which I might as well be), I walk to the table and glance down at the list:

CvC: Al's List

1. Become the most well-known kid in school
2. Pass the swimming test
3. Make someone cry
4. Retrieve a hidden piece of paper from Nathan
5. Get your first kiss
6. Give up your most prized possession
7. Stand up to Dad

I read the tasks a few times. The lava starts eating at my intestines. "I can't do any of these," I moan.

"Sure you can," Nathan says. He spins the chair around and leans against the back, toward the table. He takes another swig of orange juice. "Today's Wednesday, so you've got until next Friday morning before school. You can learn to swim by then if you work hard. You can find some random girl—or guy, heh—to smooch on. And who knows, maybe all your triumphs will make you the most well-known kid in school."

"Stand up to Dad?" I whisper.

Nathan shrugs. "Anything's possible," he says, like he's talking to someone who says the earth is made of Swiss cheese. "Wouldn't you love to tell Dad what he can do with his company dinner and his promotion? Even though he was an okay dad for years until *you* ruined it, so you deserve all the crap he gives you." (There it is again.) "But he's got to actually *know* you're standing up to him. Anyway, my turn. Give me seven tasks."

I take a deep breath and try not to imagine myself thrashing around in the pool like a blind dolphin, or going classroom to classroom shaking hands until everyone knows me as that weird kid with the handshake that feels like cold spaghetti, or . . . or making someone cry. And I know Nathan will shoot down everything I say anyway. Unless—

—unless—

"Why don't you do my list too?" I ask.

It's a stretch, but if I know Nathan, he'll at least be tempted by it. Sure enough, instead of laughing at me or calling me a goldfish, he slowly nods. "All right," he says. "I'll do the same list." And like he's reading my mind, like he's acting how I predicted he would, he says, "I didn't assume I'd be doing any of these, so I shouldn't have an unfair advantage. This way we can compete on an even ground. No loopholes. Anything you can do, I can do better."

He snatches the paper and reads it over. "Well-known kid, that's fine . . . swimming test, no big deal . . . first k—" He stops talking and turns red. When he goes back to the list, his eyes reach the bottom of the page, I guess where number seven is, and he swallows and touches the back of his head. "Fine." He slams his hands on the

29

table. "I wanted a challenge, I'm going to get one. That way when I win, it'll be because I really earned it."

He takes a pen from his pajama bottoms and writes at the top of the page: *CvC: Al's (and Nathan's) List.* "This," he says with a flourish of his pen, "is the last, final, conclusive game of CvC. Winner takes all. This I promise."

One thing about my brother: Nathan always keeps his promises. He does, however, like to play with the exact wording. I've gotten burned by loopholes in the past. This time, I need to clarify a few things. "What's stopping you from doing another game but calling it something else?"

Nathan smiles. "Skeptical, young scribe? Then I promise this will be the last game we play involving a list of items we have to accomplish, regardless of what it's called." He twirls his pen around between his fingers slowly and almost drops it onto the grass, but he's clearly too excited to care.

I think some more. "What's the hidden paper thing mean?"

"Take a sheet of computer paper, write my name on it, and hide it somewhere in the school. Has to be somewhere visible, has to be somewhere we can both access, and it can't leave the school until I find it. I'll do the same for you. Do your worst."

I sigh. "Can't I—"

"No. You can't. Unless you want me to host a big ol' coming out party."

I almost tell Nathan I'll do anything he wants as long as he doesn't tell anyone about my secret. I almost refuse to play his game. But even though he says he'll out me if I don't, he wouldn't make it that easy. He'd make me play. He wants to punish me.

The goldfish can't say no to the hyena.

My feet kick the leg of the chair. "Fine."

Nathan grins. "May the best Cole win."

Before I go to bed, I check my email. Sure enough, there's a video from Nathan waiting for me, clearly showing him setting up what looks like a little canister inside a room with a long table. *Sent this to Marcellus to prove I did it*, the email reads. *Now it's yours. Remember our pact. ;)*

How confident must he be to send this to me?

How confident is he that I'll never fight back?

When I power down my computer, I key in a new password:

iamacoward

Nathan could probably still guess that, but it sure fits.

Right when I'm about to save the change though, I see Big Green swirling around in the breeze. And I look at my sketchbook. And I think.

Not yet.

Not until my cretpoj is done.

Not until I've changed the world.

New password:

iamNOTacoward

That's something Nathan could never guess. Not in a million years.

THREE

It's a long ride to Evergreen on Thursday, and not just because 16 Werther Street is the first stop for bus 19. My head thumps in time with the bus; I swear the driver is trying to hit every single pothole on the way to school, like he gets bonus points for every dent he makes in the crossing arm. Nathan carpools with Marcellus Mitchell, his best friend (they won't let me come with them, not like I'd want to), so you'd think this would mean I could relax on the trip, but I can't. You'd have a hard time relaxing too with the threat of total social annihilation dangling over your head, like you were holding a lightning rod in a thunderstorm.

His voice floats up from the pits of my pothole-addled brain.

May the best Cole win.

So yeah, I'm a little distracted on the bus. So distracted I don't even notice someone claiming the seat next to me a few stops later. "Scooch," a voice says. I shimmy to the right and press my face against the window. I wonder if there are any families out there that could use an extra kid. I could put out an ad in the paper: *Charming twelve-year-old willing to play parts of obedient son and brother. Doesn't take up much space. Free paintings of family members' faces and bowls of fruit included in package.*

"The debate is tomorrow," Talia MacDonald says next to me. "Ask me a question."

"Uh, what debate?"

Talia shakes her head slowly. "Alan Cole, you never pay attention to anything. The debate for class president. Principal Dorset agreed to host a debate between me and Bridget Harvey. The other grades are going too. Don't you remember?"

"I guess," I say.

Talia sighs. "Well, ask me a question. I'm ready for anything. The only thing Bridget Harvey knows is what color lip gloss goes with brown eyeshadow, as if that's something you'd even need to know as class president. Ask me a question."

Another pothole slams into the bus's right front tire, making my brain do a somersault into the front of my skull. "I don't know what to ask." At least, I don't know what to ask that won't get me a Talia Lecture About a Very Important Topic.

"Alan Cole," Talia says again. "Look at me. No, not out the window—look at me. This is the most important day of seventh grade. When I get elected, I'm going to do lots of things class presidents have never even thought about doing. Miss Richter and I have been talking. I'm full of ideas for—at *me*, you muffinbrain, not at the floor—for really bringing competitive drive back to the school. Haven't you noticed nobody cares? The only ones who care are people like Madison Truman, and someone as loud and pretentious as him isn't a good role model. Competition and accountability. Statistics. Don't you agree?"

It is a small miracle, every day that goes by that I don't have to talk to Talia MacDonald.

"Ask me a question," she repeats.

I ask, "How would you become the most well-known kid in school?"

Talia leans toward me on our seat. "What kind of question is that? If you're class president, you're automatically the most well-known person in school who isn't an adult. Are you jealous of my success, Alan Cole? It's okay. When I'm elected, I'll make sure to look out for the little people like you."

She makes a stiff up-and-down motion with her neck

that's probably meant to be a nod, then at the next stop she moves a few seats down, where Rudy Brighton is sitting, probably to command him to ask her a question.

Only Talia MacDonald would treat elections for seventh grade class president like a blood sport.

Another thud.

I run my fingers over my backpack, which is nestled in between me and the window. Inside there's a folded piece of paper with *NATHAN* written on it, plus the closest thing to a "most prized possession" I have.

I don't have a clue where to hide this paper. Can't be in a classroom: a teacher would see it and throw it out. Can't be in someone's locker: Nathan wouldn't be able to get to it. As Evergreen pops up in the distance, looming tall under the sun, it hits me: where is somewhere Nathan would never go?

The band room. Nathan's played the cello for pretty much his whole life, and there's a hard law at Evergreen that all orchestra kids hate all band kids, and vice versa. He'd never be caught dead in the band room, but there's nothing *stopping* him from going there.

Maybe that's one thing he won't be able to do.

Zero down, seven to go.

The plan is to foist my most prized possession on a certain kid, but that certain kid isn't in homeroom by the time I arrive. I glance around the room. Our desks are arranged in a three-sided square, with Miss Richter's desk at the fourth side. Talia is off cornering Shariq Hakim—"Ask me a question"—and Madison Wilson Truman is reading the *Wall Street Journal*, and Miss Richter is taking a big swig from her tree-trunk-sized coffee cup, and Connor Garcia (gulp) is leaning back in his chair, looking over science notes or something. The room's abuzz with the kind of half-excited, half-exhausted energy you only get in a seventh grade classroom at seven in the morning. What would all these kids say to me if they knew? What would they call me? What would they *do* to me?

I guess I space out for a while, because next thing I know, we're all on our feet for the Pledge. I practically trip over my desk legs on the way to my feet, which of course Connor has to see. He gives me a little nod and a smile. Before I can dwell on yet another new embarrassment to add to my collection, a certain kid shows up right in the middle of the Pledge, like he's done every day since the school year started, bursting through the door out of breath.

Miss Richter, still on "to the Republic for which it stands," motions with her head, and Zack stands at the desk next to me to finish the Pledge.

Once everyone's seated (my desk decides not to

wrestle with me this time), Miss Richter makes a little notation in her roll book.

"I'm sorry," Zack says, still panting, not even bothering to whisper over the morning announcements. "I didn't mean to be late. Did you know you can see all the way down Main Street from the roof?"

"Why were you on the roof?" Rudy Brighton asks.

"I got lost."

More people laugh. Zack doesn't blush, because Zack, unlike me, has no shame.

Miss Richter puts a finger to her lips. After the announcements are over, she says, "I'm sure the roof is very fascinating, but it's off-limits to students. And is it really worth getting *another* detention over? Start showing up on time or you'll be seeing me more after school than during the day."

"Yes, ma'am," Zack says with a salute.

Once the bell rings to end homeroom, I swallow and make my move. Zack's busy squinting at the fluorescent overhead lights like he expects them to transform into pink and purple mermaids, but he perks up as soon as he notices me. "Hi," he says with a smile.

"I want you to have something," I say.

Zack gasps. "You're giving me something? Is it a blender? I've always wanted a blender. Did you know there's blenders that can make peanut butter? I always wanted to try blender butter. Since it'd be better than regular store-bought stuff, it'd be better blender butter. Better blender butter. Better bletter blatter—wait, better better batter bitter—batter batter, hey batter batter batter—" He starts cracking up, snorting really loudly.

I look around to make sure nobody is watching this debacle. "It's not a blender. It's my most prized possession."

"Wow," Zack says as we leave homeroom and head down the hall. "You're giving it to me? Really? That's awesome!"

"It's, uh," I whisper, "my lucky underwear."

Yeah, my lucky underwear is my most prized possession. You can stop laughing anytime.

When Mom bought me a pack of Hanes briefs, one pair (and only one) was bright orange. She almost threw them out, but I begged her to keep them. I mean, it's not every day you find a pair of tighty-orangies. The first day I wore them, Nathan found some new project to work on and stayed out of my hair for a whole week! I wore them on a day I found twenty bucks outside the Pine Garden bus circle. I wore them when I asked Mom for a new sketchbook two weeks ago since my old one was getting full, and she actually took me to the mall and bought me one—the same exact type as my old one. And I wore them on the first day of middle school, when

Nathan was too busy to bother me. And when he put cottage cheese in all my undies, it was only Orville Orange, smuggled in the pocket of my church pants, that escaped the cheesocide.

I even picked Orville as my prized possession over my almost-full sketchbook—my cretpoj is going to change the world, sure, but until I actually make it, it won't change much of anything. Orville, however, has saved my fanny more than once, and you can't beat that track record. I could've kept Orville until the end to give me lots of luck, but giving him away is the easiest thing on the list, so it's best if I get it over with.

Orville has one last gasp of luck to give.

I know, I know, it's silly. But Zack—and this is why I picked him—he grins. "Awesome," he says. "That's so awesome. Are you sure you want to give it up? Everyone needs a little luck."

"I'll be okay," I lie. Of course I don't tell Zack why I need to bestow this sacred artifact onto him, because then he'd want to help me with the rest of CvC, and I want that as much as I want to be swallowed by a boa constrictor. And of course Zack doesn't ask why I'm giving it to him, because he's Zack.

We pause in front of an empty classroom and out comes Orville, wrapped in three plastic bags so nobody sees I'm carrying around fluorescent undergarments. I take a deep breath, then pass it off to Zack, who takes the bag like he's King Arthur and he's found the Holy Grail.

He goes to open it, but I say, "Wait until you get home," and he nods, like we're exchanging some sacred, ancient artifact that must be opened in private (but it's really so he doesn't drop his shorts and try them on right in the middle of the hall).

We start walking again, this time in silence. Eventually Zack pulls something out of his pocket. "Check this out. This is my most prized possession." In his hand he holds . . . an ordinary-looking rock.

"Oh," I say.

"It's my special rock. My dad gave it to me. Neat, huh?"

I don't want to be rude—most prized possessions are serious business—so I nod as Zack puts the rock back in his pocket. "Yeah."

We part ways near the auditorium: beyond here is swimming class, and there are no friendly faces there. "Thanks," I say.

"I'm the one who got a great gift," Zack says. "I should be thanking you."

"Okay," I say. "You're welcome. Use Orville well."

Zack's eyes widen. "Orville?"

My cheeks flare up.

He giggles again. A loud snort rips through the air. "I'll take good care of Officer Orville. I won't let you down!"

"That's great," I mumble.

Zack puts his hand in front of his chest and dips his upper body really low, so low he almost trips. When I don't do anything, he giggles. "Handshakes are so formal. Bows are way more fun. Don't you think?"

I try to ignore the upperclassmen watching us with smirks on their faces. "How about I owe you one?"

He smiles and off he goes. Who even knows where he'll wind up, or how late he'll be. Something tells me his class isn't even down this part of the school. He skips away with Orville (yes, he literally skips), and there's an invisible thread that gets snipped when they disappear. No more lucky underwear for me. No more magic powers. No more hope that some mystical force is going to throw me an assist.

Now I'm on my own.

One down, six to go.

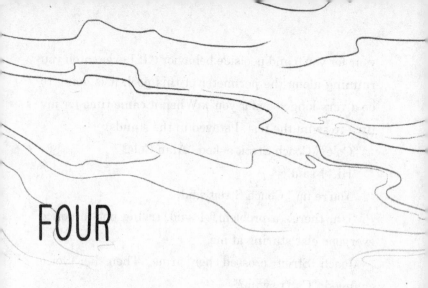

FOUR

If you've never spent the earliest parts of your morning thrashing around a cold pool and getting your lungs filled to bursting with chlorine for forty minutes and walking around the rest of the day with soggy hair smelling like the inside of a janitor's closet, you don't know what you're missing.

It's the first year swimming is required for all seventh graders (still definitely *not* calling myself a Sapling, thanks for asking). If you want to pass the class and not repeat it in eighth grade, you need to complete the exam: two lengths of the pool—one length freestyle, half-length backstroke, half-length breaststroke. We had to do this on the first day of class, after Coach Streit had explained things like locker room etiquette ("If I ever hear the sound of one towel snapping, it is going to be a very long year for you") and poolside behavior ("If I ever catch you running along the perimeter of this pool, it is going to be a very long year for you"). When it came time for my turn to swim the test, I stayed in the stands.

"Cole?" Coach Streit asked. "Alan Cole?"

"Hi," I said.

"You're up," Coach Streit said.

"Uh, there's a problem," I said, trying not to notice everyone else staring at me.

Coach Streit crossed her arms. Then her voice changed. "Can't swim?"

I nodded.

Someone laughed, and Coach Streit pivoted on her foot and barked, "There's no shame in not being able to swim. That's what we're all here to do: learn. If you don't want to learn, it is going to be a very long year for you. Fortunately for you, Cole, I've got a Shrub volunteer who's going to be spending his gym period training to be a lifeguard. He'll be working with you and helping anyone else who needs some extra practice. He's an honors student and a great worker, so you'll be in good hands."

Three guesses who that volunteer is.

If you're thinking what I think you're thinking: remember Nathan can't swim?

Today, Marcellus Mitchell raises his head in greeting as I climb into the shallow end of the pool. My brother's best (and only) friend is apparently a pretty good swimmer, even though so far he hasn't shown me much of anything except for how to get my face wet, which I already knew from my trips to Swirlieburg, Pennsylvania. Marcellus doesn't always join Nathan in games of CvC, but he's certainly never tried to stop Nathan from—

Oh crap.

He knows about CvC.

"Hold on to the edge of the pool," Marcellus says. He grips my hands and looks around for Coach Streit. "I want you to focus on one leg at a time. Spin one leg in a circle until you get tired, then do the other one, then keep going back and forth."

"That doesn't seem very helpful," I say.

"I'm like your coach," Marcellus says. "Don't you think you ought to listen to me?"

Now, I don't know much about swimming, but I know you won't get anywhere if you're trying to learn to swim by working one leg at a time. "Coach Streit's not an idiot, you know," I say.

"Neither am I," Marcellus says, his voice even. "When she comes over, work both legs. Do a lot of thrashing around. Show her how hard you're working."

"I could go to her and—"

"And what?"

He watches me, the calm to Nathan's excitable. Never takes his eyes off me. Knows what I'm going to do next.

"Yeah," I say, staring into the green pool water, "I'll listen to you."

Marcellus nods. "Good job, kid. Show everyone how hard you're working."

I lift one leg, and it hits me: he didn't mention my crush. He definitely would've made fun of me (or probably worse) if Nathan told him.

I won't tell yours as long as you cooperate, so you need to do the same. You keep me in line, I keep you in line. No loopholes. Understand?

Whatever Marcellus does or doesn't do to me, at least he's got no idea about "Vic Valentino." At least Nathan's keeping the really important end of the bargain. At least that part doesn't have any loopholes. At least the world hasn't ended yet.

The noises of the pool echo all around me: other kids doing exercises, Coach Streit blowing her whistle, splash after splash after splash. I slowly rotate one leg in the water, and Marcellus watches me work hard.

In the lunch line, I'm thinking about the colors on the cafeteria wall, ugly tans and greens that don't go together at all, and I make a mental note to never combine that particular combination of forest pastels in anything I paint, ever. I'd thought being able to see over most of the other kids would be a good thing, but if the only new thing I get to look at is vomit-colored paint, I could've done without the growth spurt. Then I hear a weird cawing noise, like a pterodactyl with bronchitis, in my ear. I jerk forward and smash into a girl who looks at me like I'm oozing toxic waste onto her expensive sneakers.

"Did you like my turtle call?" Zack asks from behind me. "I'm practicing for Oprah, my turtle. I'm trying to teach her to come on command. But you're not a turtle, so it probably scared you, huh?" He laughs so hard spit flies out of his mouth and onto my shirt.

"I was terrified," I say in a flat voice.

"Hey," Zack says as we move up in line, "I wanted you to have something. Well, I still do, so I guess I should say 'I want you to have something,' not 'I wanted you to have something.' Or maybe it's 'I am wanting you to have something.' I don't know. Verbs are confusing. I wish we didn't have verbs in English, and we could be like, 'I you to something.' I think that'd get the point across." He takes a breath. "So, I you to something, Alan." He giggles. Again.

We move up farther in line. "What is it?" I ask, even though I'm not sure I want to know.

"You me something, I you something too. That's No-Verb for 'you gave me something, I'll give you something too.'" He fishes around in his pocket and pulls out a big clump of tiny, rubber-banded—

"Are those fortunes from fortune cookies?" I ask.

Zack nods. "I collect them and bring them to school sometimes. Me and my mom get Chinese food from this takeout place up the road a lot, and they always have the best fortunes. Go on. Pick one."

"Pick a fortune?"

"You need some luck, right? Go ahead. Close your eyes and pick one."

Sighing, I close my eyes and grab the first one. It says, in text clearly written on a typewriter older than me:

Where do babies come from?

I turn the paper over. "Where's the fortune?"

Zack looks at what I picked and starts cracking up with loud snorts. "Oh, you got the best one! That's actually a fortune I got last week. Can you believe it?"

"This isn't a fortune," I say. "It's a question."

"Questions can be fortunes."

Whether he's right or not—he's not—something tells me "Where do babies come from?" should only go on a fortune cookie in very specific situations, and I don't think I fit any of them.

Zack keeps going on about some of the other fortunes

he's gotten at this place, like, "Buy off-brand tissues," "It was very loud in here, wasn't it?" and one that was just the number nineteen, which I'm pretty sure is potassium on the periodic table. Who knew fortune cookies could help you learn science?

When we get to the Unstable Table, Madison is sipping his bottled water with a straw and picking at a Tupperware container of leafy greens. "Salad," he says with his face scrunched up. "Mom isn't being very subtle."

"Maybe she wants you to have a balanced meal," Zack says, burying his face in his meatball sandwich.

Madison continues, "She also wants me to go to the private health club she and Dad belong to, so I can get in shape. It's ridiculous."

"You don't think you'll lose weight?" Zack spits bits of meat as he talks.

Madison shakes his head. "Of course I will. I'm Madison Wilson Truman. I'm going to lose so much weight, I'll be a stick. The happiest stick boy in Petal Fields." He pokes a bit of kale with his fork.

I swallow a big bite of last night's leftover pasta and try not to look at Connor slugging the guy beside him on the arm at the next table, try not to wonder what he'd think if he found out how I really feel. All this worrying can't be good for me. If Nathan's goal was to make me turn gray and wrinkled by the end of the week, so far he's doing a pretty good job of it.

Of course, right now is when Connor notices me staring. He nods at me and smiles. I hold my lunch tray over my eyes in a panic. Then I realize, oh my God, I'm *holding a lunch tray over my face*, but by that point he's stopped looking. Another potentially embarrassing encounter upgraded to definitely embarrassing, courtesy of Alan Cole.

"Hmph," Madison huffs, swallowing a soggy piece of kale like it's trying to claw its way out of his throat. "I need someone to tutor. Nobody wants to learn physics from a twelve-year-old. That's their loss."

"Do you know a lot about physics?" Zack asks.

Madison clears his throat. "This and that. I know a good bit about the coefficient of fiction."

Zack nods. "Wow. That's really zen."

(My eye twitches so rapidly the *friction* would be enough to start a fire. But I keep my mouth shut.)

As if reading my thoughts, Madison turns to me and says, "Alan, give me a list of all the classes you take and rank them in order from 'most likely to need Madison's help with' to 'I'm fine, thank you much.'"

"I'm fine, thank you much," I say.

"I could use some help with science," Zack says. "I don't get the time travel stuff."

Madison narrows his eyes. "There is no time travel in science class."

Zack exhales. "Well, that explains that then."

"Honestly," Madison says, shaking his head. Then he sighs. "Sometimes I wish I had a brother or sister. Someone to take the pressure off. It must be nice."

"I wouldn't know," Zack says. "Alan's got an older brother though, right?"

I look up. How did he—

"I saw him hide in an empty room waiting for you the other day," Zack says with a shrug. "It doesn't look like you like him very much."

Now I look back down at my food, even though my appetite's starting to fade. "I'd rather not talk about him."

"I've certainly never heard of him," Madison says. "He must be quiet. Runs in the family, I suppose." He chuckles.

"He's not quiet to me," I grumble before I can stop myself.

"He seems like a fun enough guy," Zack says.

I open my mouth, but then I can't close the stupid thing. "He's fun, sure. He has plenty of fun making my life miserable any way he can, like those stupid CvC games, where he had me doing all kinds of humiliating things, and now he's making me play a new game with even worse things to do and there's *stakes* and I had to give you my lucky underwear and if I don't play along—"

I take a deep breath and slide back on my seat. I actually put my hand over my mouth to keep it shut.

"Wow," Madison says, eyes wide.

"S-Sorry," I stammer, looking for a black hole to crawl into.

"Games?" Zack asks. "What kind of games?"

"Forget I said anything." I duck my head.

Zack moves in closer. "I want to play a game. Can I play?"

"No," I say, as loud as I think I've ever said anything. "No way. If Nathan knew I had help, he'd go after you. I'm not letting that happen—" I almost say "again," but I stop myself.

"Does your brother have help?" Zack asks.

Spin one leg in a circle until you get tired, then do the other one, then keep going back and forth. "Maybe."

"Alan, come on," Zack says. "You gave me your lucky underwear and I gave you a fortune. That makes us best friends now."

"You took his underwear?" Madison asks. "Why does that not surprise me?"

"What sort of stuff do you have to do?" Zack asks. "I want to help you win the game. Come on, Alan."

I sigh. "No. Forget I said anything."

"Hang on." Madison dramatically pushes away his salad. "I could help you with this. Do any of these challenges involve the coefficient of fiction?"

"Yeah!" Zack says. "We can do it together. We'll team up, combine our powers, and be unstoppable! Like hurricanes, or angry moms!"

The tide is turning. The waves are crashing down, whirlpools swirling, storms beating against the rocks. "Why are you doing this?" I ask.

"I already told you," Zack says. "We're best friends."

"We're not—"

"All right," Madison says. "I'll help."

Zack starts hollering and spinning in his seat.

I know I've lost this fight. When you lose as often as I do, you know when it's coming, and you know when you have to accept a big, fat *L* in your record books.

Zack reaches out a hand to stop his spinning, but he overcompensates and almost falls off the seat. Madison whispers to me, "Don't worry. I'll lead you to victory. I'll show the world what I can do. You'll be in good hands." He rubs his hands together and chuckles under his breath.

Once Zack recovers, he leans into the table, a big grin plastered on his face. "Okay, Game Master Alan. Deputy Zack and Officer Orville reporting for duty. What's the first thing we need to do?"

I look at Zack Kimble, hedgehog hair zigzagging from his eager, bright-eyed face, and I look at Madison Truman, closely cropped buzz cut highlighting his determined, ready gaze, and I imagine myself, Alan Cole, parted black hair swooshing down over my forehead. Three faces, dying to be captured in a cretpoj, a cretpoj that won't be put on hold by any brothers or their games. The Unstable Table lurches a little as I rest my elbows on the edge.

I blow a bit of hair out of my eyes, and I say, "Help me become the most well-known kid in school."

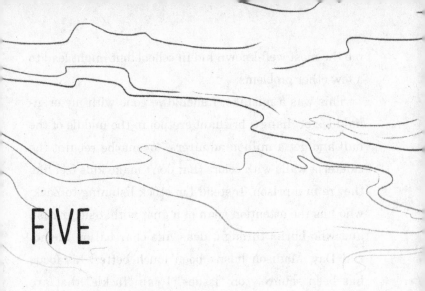

FIVE

"No."

"Come on. It wouldn't be that embarrassing."

"Um, yeah, it would."

"Well, okay, maybe it would be *at first*, but I'm sure you'd get used to being naked in school. It's like wearing a bathing suit, except without the suit, and with more goose bumps."

It's been like this ever since I told them about the game: Zack ping-ponging suggestions for how to become well-known, and me serving them back with flat-out *no*s. The naked idea isn't even the worst thing he's come up with. Madison had to convince him spray-painting a big mural of myself on the door would get me expelled ("I thought you liked art!"), which would technically make me the most well-known kid in school, but might lead to a few other problems.

This was a mistake. I should've gone with my original idea of "hang a brilliant cretpoj in the middle of the hall and get a million admirers," or maybe repaint the cafeteria walls with colors that don't make kids feel like they're in a prison. Instead I'm stuck listening to Zack, who has the attention span of a gnat with a sugar rush and who burns through ideas like charcoal on Memorial Day. Madison hasn't been much better: his focus has been squarely on "issues" I can "tackle" that are "hot-button and relevant to today's youth." Thus far he's suggested special interest lobbyists, HMOs, and insider trading. I don't even know what any of that stuff *is*.

After he wouldn't answer my question about what a lobbyist actually does apart from "sit in a lobby," I'm pretty sure he doesn't know what any of it is either.

I'd be better off tackling this like I decided to tackle swimming: blunder around and eventually, hopefully, stumble into the answer.

At least then nobody would get hurt.

After lunch is social studies. As we walk into Miss Richter's room, Madison claps me on the back and says, "You should feel honored. You have a great opportunity to say something important, something so—"

"Madison," Jenny Cowper says as she walks by, "you

wouldn't know the first thing about being important."

Madison puffs out his cheeks. "I know plenty of things, and I can give a report on all of them."

Jenny smirks. "Whatever."

I escape Madison's clutches and sit at my desk. Right when I think I'm safe for now, Zack sits next to me and blurts out, "Hey, I thought of something: you already gave me your underwear, so it's like you're halfway to naked already!" He grins and gives me a thumbs-up.

I huddle into my desk and pray everyone stops looking at me soon.

"All right there, Alan?" somebody asks. I look up and a little catch forms at the base of my throat, because my other desk neighbor is asking, and that neighbor happens to be Connor.

"Uh, y-yeah, hi," I stumble.

Connor smiles his big smile, chews his spearmint-scented gum, and flips through his notebook, leaving me with more butterflies than a cavern of cocoons. I try to ignore the heat huffing through my face and bury my nose in whatever random stack of papers I yank out of my backpack.

It's not like this is the first time Connor's said anything to me. We went to Pine Garden Elementary together, after all, and since we were both in the advanced classes, we got paired together a lot. But it wasn't until last year that I started getting really nervous around him—more nervous than I usually got with people. Connor started getting taller and he sprouted muscles all over the place and his voice got a little deeper, and his smile . . . I never noticed before then how big his smile was.

I didn't start putting the pieces together until recently, hence the search history Nathan found. I've heard that a lot of kids my age start questioning things and don't really figure stuff out until they get older, so this could all still be up in the air for me. But I'll tell you something: Between you and me, I like Connor more than I've ever liked any girl. And there's definitely been other guys, and no girls, I've looked at and thought . . . okay, you get the point.

When we're all seated, Miss Richter takes a gulp from her silo-sized coffee thermos. "Okay," she says. "Today I've got a handout—yes, Madison?"

Madison's hand had rocketed up into the air the millisecond after Miss Richter had set down her thermos. "Miss Richter, I found an error in our textbook." He holds up the gargantuan tome—*Discovering America*, eighth edition—then smashes it down on his desk. The loud crashing noise makes me, along with everybody else in the room, jump. "Page fifty-six," Madison continues. "It says President James Madison's 'accomplishments were not as grand in scope as those of the prior president,

Thomas Jefferson.' When I read that, you can understand, I was simply outraged. I've prepared a report on the accomplishments of President Madison for the class's benefit."

Groans fill the room.

"James Madison was a boring president," Talia says, a few seats down. "Thomas Jefferson wrote the Declaration of Independence."

"Which James Madison also signed," Madison says.

Talia leans toward Madison. "Signed and wrote are two different things, Madison Truman. It's a little disappointing you don't know that."

I'm busy looking down at my desk, almost putting my fingers in my ears, when Madison says, "Alan, back me up."

Everyone in the room looks at me.

"Uh, what?"

"Back me up," Madison repeats. "Camp Madison. We'll defend our fort against Camp Jefferson any day. Isn't that right?"

I slide down my desk. Talia glares daggers through my face. Connor watches me, chewing his gum slowly. "Uh . . . um . . ."

"Unbelievable," Talia says, punching each syllable in the stomach. "Boys against girls? Fine. *I'll* take Miss Richter. Our teacher, in case you've forgotten. And she says Camp Madison is flimsy at best."

"You're flimsy at best," Madison grumbles. "Alan? Back me up."

I wish with all my might to evaporate into water vapor and float out the window. Zack, next to me, is zoned out, mouth open as he gazes outside, probably watching something amazing, like a bird fly, or a tree sway. Connor's still looking at me.

"That's enough," Miss Richter finally says. "Debates are fine, but no name-calling. I expect better of you. You especially, Talia, since you're running for class president."

Talia sticks her nose into the air.

"But Miss Richter," Madison whines. "People need to know the truth. Once I give the report, everyone will see."

"There's no need for a report," Miss Richter says. "Sometimes—and this goes for all of you—you have to accept that people are going to disagree with you. I'm not letting you make a speech right now, Madison, but when the next project comes around, you can. How does that sound?"

Madison looks at Talia, who smirks. "Peachy," he says. Then he looks at me and scowls. Like I did something wrong. Like I somehow betrayed Camp Madison, which I'm pretty sure isn't a thing that exists, and I'm also pretty sure there are about three or four presidents with *grander accomplishments* than Thomas Jefferson, and James Madison isn't one of them.

But telling that to Madison Wilson Truman is like telling a kid named Bruce Wayne he's doomed to a life of happiness and crime-free, non-bat-related things. Madison shoots me one last glance and runs a hand over his hair.

When the papers Miss Richter passes out get to Zack's desk, Zack spins around and faces me. "Hey," he whispers to me. "What did I miss?"

"Pair up with your study partners," Miss Richter says, returning to her desk. "Go over the worksheet and help each other out. This class needs to get more comfortable with the idea of teamwork."

I look at Zack to my left, but Zack's already been unwillingly claimed by Julie Linder, who looks about as thrilled as if she'd been told to drink raw sewage. That leaves the kid to my right.

"You and me, Alan," Connor says, taking his gum out. "Just like old times, huh?"

"Y-Yeah," I stammer. I open *Discovering America* and focus on one page so I don't have to look at my study partner.

"Dude," Connor says. "We're doing right after the Revolutionary War, and that's a picture of Martin Luther

King. I think you went a little too far."

I nod. "Sorry."

He smiles. "Man, I'm glad you're my study partner. You really helped me out a lot at Pine Garden. Not gonna lie, sometimes this stuff makes me feel like an idiot, y'know?"

"You're not an idiot."

"Heh," Connor laughs. "You're, like, the nicest guy in the world, you know that?"

I swear my entire body is about to combust. I try to swallow but there's a bowling ball wedged in my esophagus.

"I hope we're all working on our assignments and not gossiping about squirrels," Miss Richter says to the class, looking right at Zack.

"But they're so cool," Zack says. "They have cute little cheeks, and—"

"Save it for later, Zack," Miss Richter says. "Focus on your worksheets."

Zack whispers, "We'll catch up on squirrels some other time," and Julie Linder rolls her eyes.

We spend most of the class completing the worksheet. I come up with all the answers, not because Connor is slacking off, but because I know the material better than he does. When it comes time for the last question,

Connor says, "Hey, let me do this one. You've been doing all the work."

"It's okay," I say. "I don't mind."

"I've got to earn my keep," Connor says with a smile. "'What was the central principle behind the Monroe Doctrine?' I remember going over this in class."

I open my mouth, but Connor says, "Take a load off, man. Let me do some heavy lifting. Uh, the Monroe Doctrine is that thing that says the US could do whatever they wanted in North America, right?"

"Something like that," I say. "It said we were free to colonize North America without Europe getting involved, and in exchange we'd stay out of European colonies."

"Oh yeah," Connor says.

I start writing down the answer. "It's fine. You were close."

"It's so weird though. Why wouldn't Europe come over and be like, forget this doctrine or whatever, we're taking Texas. What's stopping them?"

I put my pencil to my lips for a second. Maybe America knew a secret of Europe's, and Europe knew a secret of America's, and they agreed to never tell the rest of the world if they both played along. "Beats me."

Connor smiles. "I feel better about not knowing stuff if there's something the great Alan Cole doesn't know."

"Pftyleeargh," I say, spitting all over *Discovering America.*

"Huh?" Connor writes down the answer on his own sheet. "You say something?"

"N-Nothing," I say, wiping my mouth off as fast as I can. "Don't worry about it."

When the bell rings, I hand in my worksheet to Miss Richter. "Are you okay from earlier?" she whispers as other kids bring up their papers. "You looked like you were ready to melt during that argument."

"Oh, I'm fine," I say, blushing a little.

She watches me carefully, but anything else she might say gets cut off as Madison stomps over to me, grumbling, "Why didn't you back me up?"

"Uh," I say, but I can't think of anything else, because honestly, what else would you even say? Sorry for not rushing to your defense in the World's Stupidest Argument Contest, and by the way, congrats on winning?

Madison sighs. "I'm sorry. I probably shouldn't have put you on the spot like that. I thought that maybe, for once, somebody would—"

"Alan," Zack calls from outside the room. "Come here."

Like somebody knocked the wind out of him, Madison stops talking. He clears his throat, nods stiffly, and leaves the classroom. I look back at Miss Richter, whose eyes dart away from me the second I stare at her, and I follow Madison.

Zack stands by the empty, broken vending machine outside Miss Richter's room. That thing's been out of order since the school year started, with no chips or candy to be found inside, its hollow holders barren and lifeless. There's nothing sadder than an empty vending machine. Zack's looking at it like there's something inside—

Hang on. There is something inside.

We make our way closer. There are a few kids hovering around the machine; some of them are whispering. Zack gives me a wide-eyed, baby-fawn look, and I take a closer peek.

It's a piece of paper. Dirty, with plenty of stains all over it. But clearly visible through the stains, written in black Sharpie, are the words:

FOR AL

;)

My stomach tries to leap out of my throat. How in the—

"They should really get that thing removed," Madison scoffs. "Come on, we'll be late for class."

Zack still watches me. Then he grips the glass window of the vending machine and tries to pull it off.

"What are you doing?" Madison gasps. "That's destruction of school property! I said I wanted it removed, but you don't have to—"

"No good," Zack says. "We need to get that paper. Right, Alan?"

Madison starts, "Why would—" He stops. "You didn't tell me you liked being called Al."

"That's because I don't." My voice comes out flat, as empty as the vending machine.

"I get it." Zack peers through the vending machine. "This is part of the game. This is something else you have to do to beat your brother. Right, Alan?"

"You need to tell us everything about this game," Madison says, crossing his arms.

"And we need to figure out how to get that paper out," Zack says. "Right?"

The rules said I had to be able to get to the paper. There's no way I can get to it without taking apart or breaking into the machine. It's too high up for me to reach if I stick my arm through the slot at the bottom. He's cheating. It's impossible.

Right?

But if he's cheating, then I can tell everyone about his stink bomb escapades. Unless that's part of his trap too, like he wants me to tell everyone, because it'll somehow make me look worse, and—and—

I always keep my promises.

"Alan," Madison says slowly. "What happens if you lose this game?"

I look at the vending machine. At that dirty piece of paper. He probably made it gross, with stains and holes, just to make me not want to take it, just to taunt me— and it's that thought that sparks something, or maybe it's looking at myself in the glass, with hair in my eyes, or maybe it's Connor's voice echoing *the great Alan Cole* in my head.

Whatever it is, it makes me think, *I am NOT a coward.*

Whatever it is, it makes me say to Madison, "It doesn't matter, because I'm going to win."

When I say it, I almost—almost—believe it.

And almost is better than not at all.

Zack pumps his fist into the air and yells "Ohhhhh!" all up and down the hall until a teacher tells him to knock it off.

"You still owe me an explanation," Madison says on the way to science. "A full explanation."

"Are you sure you want to help me?" I ask.

Madison holds himself up to his full height (which puts him at about my throat). "This is going to be my crowning achievement. You'll not only become well-known, you'll do so many things, and I'll be right there behind you every step of the way."

"Taking all the credit," I say.

He clears his throat. "You make it sound so terrible."

"Sorry," I mumble. "It was a joke."

"Hmm," Madison says, "I didn't know you joked."

"Neither did I."

"It's a good style for you. I say keep it."

I nod. "Maybe I will."

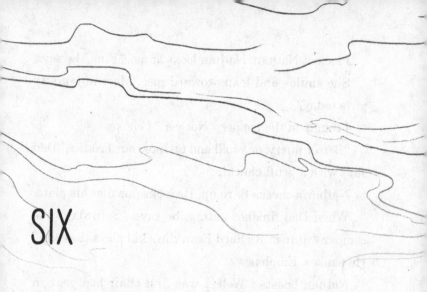

SIX

The wooden clock in the kitchen seeps over the dinner table, its rhythmic clanking echoing in my skull along with the scraping utensils and the distant hum of the fridge. Mom's chicken stew is tasty, and bits of hot pepper flakes she sprinkled on top practically leave scorch marks as they dribble down my throat, but I barely notice it.

I'm thinking about the principles of design Mrs. Colton went over today in art class, and how the scene in front of me would look if I painted it. Where would the emphasis be? On the clock? At the head of the table? On the carefully prepared food? Where would the movement flow? What patterns would be repeated?

"How's school going?" Mom asks halfway through dinner.

I look at Nathan. Nathan looks at me. "Fine," he says.

She smiles and leans toward me. "Meet any pretty girls today?"

I cough on the pepper. "Not yet," I choke.

"Better hurry, or you'll end up like your brother," Dad says with a gruff chuckle.

Nathan's cheeks flare up. He looks down at his plate.

When Dad finishes eating, he says, "Saturday's the company dinner. Richard Franklin's kid plays the cello." He pauses. Emphasis.

Nathan boasts, "Well, I was first chair last year in the Evergreen Middle School orchestra, and the orchestra is going to perform a piece I've written this year."

(Stretching the truth a bit there—Nathan did write some piece of music, but the orchestra teacher only said he'd "consider putting it on." But he did get first chair.)

Dad doesn't react to Nathan's bragging. Instead, he asks Mom, "Got your good dress back from the cleaners?"

Mom nods. "I got a few other things cleaned too. Some sets of church clothes, and—"

"Sure it still fits?" Dad asks.

The heat and silence fill every space of the kitchen. Finally, as Dad stares unblinkingly at his wife, Mom looks down at what's left of her bowl of stew. Downward movement. "It will fit," she says.

Dad looks at me. "What sports do you play?"

Again: I don't play any sports. That's not why he's asking. "I run long distance, I play shortstop, and I'd show you my bilateral kick if I remembered to bring my soccer ball."

Dad's eyes narrow. "Uh, bicycle kick, bicycle," I stammer, but he raises his head, and I freeze.

Upward movement.

He downs his water in one gulp and places the glass, very gently, on the table. He stares at me, unblinking. I don't move. Nobody moves. Only the clock moves. "This is what all that art stuff gets you?" he asks me. "No common sense. Nobody's impressed by artists."

Nathan's elbow slides off the table, sending his spoon plummeting to the floor. "Something you want to say, little pig?" Dad asks his eldest son. Pattern.

"No," Nathan grumbles. "No, Father."

Pigs like to roll around in their own slop and make huge messes everywhere they go. But I'd still rather be a pig than a goldfish. At least people care enough about pigs to eat them.

"Our little pig," Dad says. "You get everything handed to you because you've got brains. But sometimes you can't get by with just brains. You've got to work hard. You don't know that yet."

"I know some things," Nathan whispers.

Dad raises his head again. Outward movement. "Like what?"

I hunch into my chair, folding into myself. Nathan looks down at the table. "I know none of our family ever visits us," he whispers.

I grip the edges of my chair. Nathan's gone too far, and judging by how he actually inches his chair away from the table, he knows it too. Dad goes deathly still. Mom says to me, "Why don't you show us what you're painting—"

"We have no family." Dad's words cut across the ice like a chainsaw. "It's just us. That's how it's always been and that's how it's always going to be. Family, family, family. Aren't I enough family for you, little pig?" He grabs his empty glass of water and gazes into it like it holds the answers to some abstract puzzle. Abruptly he stands up and fumes out of the kitchen, his shadow lurking behind.

Dad always shuts down whenever someone, usually Nathan, brings up family or the past. Millions of Coles in the world, even one or two at Evergreen, and none of them are related to us? I don't know if we have any grandparents, or aunts or uncles or cousins. All I know is Dad refuses to talk about them, and Mom's not offering any answers.

Mom goes to the fridge and returns with a glass of

orange juice. She places it in front of Nathan, wringing her hands. He stares at it for a few seconds, then downs it in one gulp and walks upstairs. He sort of looks like . . . how I look during CvC season.

Pattern.

Mrs. Colton says, "Life imitates art." I wonder if she had her own 16 Werther Street growing up, and if she ever made her own cretpoj out of it.

I stare at the last page of my old sketchbook, brush in hand, trying to put all those highfalutin principles of design to use and come up with at least a rough draft of a face.

Who should it be? What face could I paint that will change the world? I spend so much time thinking about who to paint that I don't paint anyone.

Maybe the problem is I don't *want* to paint a face. Maybe I'm forcing it. Maybe I should go back downstairs and paint the dishes in the sink, or open my window and paint Big Green again.

I don't want to give up. Not yet. I don't want to run away from every problem.

Right when I'm about to start on the oval-shaped outline for a head, any head, my sketchbook gets snatched out of my hands and held above my head.

Crap.

"Sorry to interrupt." Nathan dangles all my work from the past year over my head carelessly, like he could toss it out the window any second. "I wanted to say hi."

"Hi," I whine. If I play up how irritated I am with the interruption, Nathan will go easier on me. Hopefully.

My brother tosses the sketchbook in the corner of my room, then he starts pacing back and forth. "Y'know," he says, "I was thinking. I wonder if you'll still be able to paint your little paintings after CvC. How can you get your mystical inspiration if everyone hates you? Where's the beauty of the world or whatever?"

I don't say anything.

"Of course," he continues, hopping onto my bed and bouncing up and down, "that's assuming you, my little Colette, don't do more tasks than me. Which, let's be real here, you won't." He starts attempting tricks as he jumps, almost falling off the bed with each rotation of his body.

Now, I'm a lot of things. According to Dad I'm a goldfish, according to my almost-computer password I'm a coward, and according to Connor I'm the nicest guy in the world. But one thing I've never been is reckless. I'm a survivor. I always look out for myself.

Except now. Now, because I am a complete moron, I say, "I've done one task already. How many have you done?"

He stops bouncing.

I take a deep breath. "I'm sure you're still going to win."

Nathan walks over to my closet, right where my church clothes are kept. He fishes around inside the pants pocket. "Huh," he says. "You gave them up."

"How did—"

"I always knew," he says. "At least I did after you still had underwear after the Great Cottage Cheese Incident. Haven't you figured it out yet, Al? I know everything about you. You can't surprise me. So you gave up your most prized possession. So what? That was the easiest one. Did you dump them in the trash? The garbage can's probably all Day-Glo now."

"I gave them to someone. That's what the rules say we have to do."

A snicker cuts across Nathan's throat, then it rips into a full-on cackle. "Are you serious? You actually gave someone your underwear? A real, living human being took your underwear? The rules say give *up*, not give *away*. You could've thrown them in the fireplace for all I care."

Speaking of fire, that's what's spreading across my face right now.

"We're on the honor system," Nathan continues. "Remember? Mutual secrets? You're so stupid, Al. I can't believe you got someone to take your *underwear!*" Hyena's laughter surrounds me, cuts into my blood.

"Oh yeah?" I ask, rearing up for a fight. But I've got nothing. Burned again by exact wording.

Nathan rests his hands on his knees, almost dizzy from laughing so hard. "Anyway, that was the easiest one. You won't be able to do anything else. I'll breeze through mine like nobody's business, like usual."

Time to change the subject. "What's your most prized possession?"

"None of your business. But you'll know when I give it *up*. Did you find my paper yet?"

My back goes stiff, and Nathan laughs. "Excellent," he says. "Remember, you've got to actually take the paper, not just find it. Yes, young Padawan, you're more than capable of getting that paper out of the vending machine without taking it apart or smashing the glass. I promise."

When Nathan leaves my room, I don't go for my sketchbook right away. I sit at my desk, thinking. Is this what a little confidence does? Makes you turn stupid? Into a stupid goldfish?

By my keyboard is Zack's "fortune." If fortune cookies want to ask questions, they should ask good ones, not ones about where babies come from. They should ask, what's your most prized possession? What would it take for you to give it up? They should ask, how do you break into a vending machine? (Or they could *tell* you how. That'd be fine too.)

I need some water after this whole mess of an evening, so I head downstairs. There's low talking from the living room. I peer around the corner and Mom's on the couch, her cell phone in her hand, a muted TV in the background. She's speaking to the person on the other end, probably Denise, one of her friends from church. (Denise has kids around my and Nathan's age, but Nathan scared them off years ago.) I can't hear most of what she says, but one phrase really sticks out:

"I've lost it all."

When I shift my feet, the floorboards creak. She looks up, mutters a hasty good-bye to Denise, and watches me from across the room. "You should be in bed," she says.

"I got thirsty," I say.

She folds her hands over her lap. Standing in the living room doorway I remember how she smiled at me when I came home with a gold star for a great drawing, and how she laughed when I told a knock-knock joke I overheard at recess, and how she hugged me when I fell and scraped my knee. Her face had fewer lines then. I also remember how light a sleeper she is, how she hears everything that goes on between me and Nathan, how she's backed away from me, left me raw and naked against the hawk's talons. How all the glasses of orange juice in the world can't wash down the acid brewing below our throats.

A fortune cookie should ask, what makes somebody disappear? What makes them accept a painful situation, shut down, retreat away from the people they care about? How do you bring someone you love back from the depths?

Can you?

"Get some sleep," Mom says. "Tomorrow's another day." She smiles a worn smile and turns back to the TV.

I've lost it all.

I stand there for Lord knows how long, watching her, zonked out in front of the news. I don't know what I'm looking for. I just watch.

Emphasis.

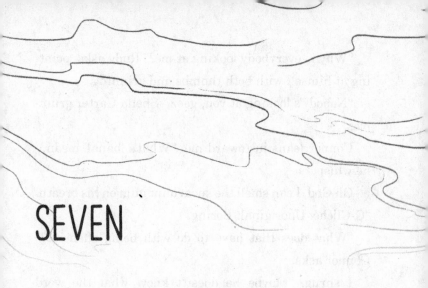

SEVEN

"And once again, I would like to remind all students that toilet paper is to be used for bathroom purposes only, and not for decorating your locker or book bag."

All around me, snickers. Rudy Brighton yells, "What if we have an accident in the middle of class?"

"Guess you'll need to buy a new book bag," Miss Richter says. She takes a sip from her thermos. "Now be quiet and pay attention."

From the loudspeaker, Principal Dorset's voice blares out in all its grainy quality. "Finally, today we have our class president elections for Saplings, Sprouts, and Shrubs. The candidates for each grade will take part in a debate, with questions posed by their peers. I want to stress how we must all be on our best behavior. Do not ask questions which are lewd, offensive, or banal."

"Why is everybody looking at me?" Rudy asks, pointing at himself with both thumbs and grinning.

"Nobody's looking at you, geez," Sheila Carter grumbles.

Connor leans in toward me. "What's 'banal' mean?" he whispers.

Oh God, I can smell the spearmint gum on his breath. "C-Cliché. Unoriginal. Boring."

"What does that have to do with being offensive?" Connor asks.

I shrug. "Maybe he doesn't know what the word means."

Connor laughs, which makes Miss Richter sigh. "Can't we keep it together for one round of morning announcements?" she asks.

"I don't know, Miss Richter," Rudy says, "you'd have to be pretty morning announce-mental to not find this stuff funny."

Sheila moans. "Please kill me."

When the announcements are done, Miss Richter stands up. "Let's all wish Talia the best of luck against Bridget Harvey today."

Talia's eyes look like they're going to set anything in their path on fire. "I don't need luck. I'm going to crush her."

"If you win, can you fix the water fountains?" Zack

asks. (He made it to homeroom at the last possible second today, picking leaves out of his bird's-nest hair. Don't ask.) "All the ones I've used, the water barely comes out, it's like a little trickle, and it tastes stale, like you wouldn't think water could get stale, but all our water fountains really taste like water that's been left in plastic bottles in somebody's warm car at the beach for the whole summer. You should make that a top priority. 'Talia Fountain-Fixing MacDonald.' I'd vote for you."

"I'm not answering that," Talia says. "Do I have to answer that? I'm not answering that."

Rudy blows a raspberry. "Some debater. You should run for Congress. Hey, did you know the opposite of Congress is *progress*? Get it? It's funny because—"

Miss Richter cuts him off with a wave of her hand. "Be respectful, and don't make bad jokes. Set the bar high, Rudy."

When the bell rings, Zack turns to me and says, "So here's how you're going to save my life. We'll find a giant pendulum from somewhere, maybe in the theater closet, and I'll tie myself up underneath, and you'll rush in heroically and save the day before I'm sliced into little Zack cubes. Or crushed by *Discovering America*. Sound good?"

I sigh. "Do I want to know?"

"How else are you going to get well-known?" he asks.

"It makes complete sense. Save a life, make the front page of the *Evergreen Leaf Blower*, and you'll be Mr. Well-Known. Your brother can't compete with that!" He makes two thumbs-up and wiggles them above his head.

"I'm not doing that," I say flatly, like I've said to everything else he's suggested.

"Come on, haven't you ever wanted to be a superhero? Now's your chance. You can be Alan Man. Or Swimmer Dude. Yeah, that's it—I'll pretend to drown, and you save my life. Bravissimo!"

"I can't swim. Remember?"

Zack's thumbs in the air slowly deflate. "Oh yeah."

I told Zack and Madison everything about CvC yesterday, except the stakes—as far as they're concerned, I won't be able to do any art for a year if I lose, and not . . . the actual punishment. Now they know what I have to do, what I'm up against. They said they'd still try to help me win, and I wasn't sure if I should've said "thank you" or "what size paper bag would best fit my head?" Madison got excited about coaching me on how to get my first kiss. I think I'd rather get kissing advice from a hungry lion.

"Gentlemen," Madison says as we all exit homeroom. "I've got it. I know how Alan is going to become well-known."

"Is he going to save your life too?" Zack asks. "I've got

dibs on the pendulum. That's going to be sooooo cool." He holds a hand to his forehead like he's going to faint from excitement.

Madison looks at Zack like he's trying to scrape the guy off his shoe, then he focuses on me again. "You're going to ask a question at the debate today."

"At the debate?" My stomach churns. "In front of all the seventh graders?"

"Not just *Saplings*. The other grades will be there too. That's why it's perfect. You'll ask a deep and meaningful question and bring attention to a serious problem—"

"Like fixing the water fountains!" Zack yells.

"I can't." My voice drowns in the crowd of kids in the halls. "I can't do it."

Madison stops walking, reaches up, and grabs my shoulders; Zack promptly crashes into Madison's back. "Alan, listen to me," Madison says, jerking his body away from Zack's. "You can do this. You have to do this. If you ask the right question, people won't just remember you: they'll remember you as a hero. I'll brainstorm questions for you to ask. You're in good hands!" He rubs his "good hands" together and disappears.

Of all the horrible misdeeds Nathan's forced me to perform for CvC, public speaking wasn't one of them. I've made a horse's keister out of myself lots of times, but getting up in front of a room and saying something?

I don't even think Nathan could've made me do that.

And yet, here I am.

Like it or not, it's a good idea: ask a good question at the debate, in front of the whole school, and everyone will know me . . . as some mumbly, tall, white kid. Would it be enough to make me well-known?

After Nathan left last night, I couldn't paint at all. Not even the outline of a head. If I lose this, will I ever paint again? Will I ever be relaxed enough, in tune enough, to do anything?

That old wooden clock of Dad's in the kitchen keeps ticking. I have a week left, and time doesn't stop for anyone, certainly not Alan Cole.

I stop walking, trying to catch my thoughts, and Zack promptly crashes into my back.

After swimming class ("Today you're going to move your arms around a little, one at a time, and make sure you really look like you're working hard when Coach Streit walks by"), it's time for the assembly. Trying to pack all of Evergreen into one auditorium is hard enough without all the noise that comes with it. It's like herding yodeling cattle.

After I check in with Miss Richter, Madison motions me over to a seat with an impatient flutter of his hand. "I've been brainstorming," he practically yells in my ear.

"I've come up with several amazing ideas."

"I can't do this," I mumble.

I don't know if Madison can't hear me or if he's ignoring me; either way he keeps talking. "You need to ask something hard-hitting, something that will make the candidates really stop to think about the issues students face. Here's a list." He pulls a sheet of paper out of his backpack; my eyes bulge out at the writing covering *both sides of the paper*. "Let's see here . . . newer supplies for classrooms—I have a chart outlining some examples . . . field trips to museums and art exhibits instead of the local paper mill, which could still be exciting, given the right approach . . . updated computer supplies . . . outdated and inaccurate textbooks that incorrectly portray James Madison in an unfavorable light—that's one you should definitely consider—"

"I can't do this," I repeat. The stage spotlight is on two podiums, and Principal Dorset is talking to both Talia and Bridget Harvey. Talia keeps glancing out at the crowd while Bridget twirls her hair. I guess Principal Dorset tells Bridget to take the gum out of her mouth, because she spits it into a little wrapper, then waves to somebody in the front row.

"—and that one's a little confrontational, but you'll need to be firm if people want to remember you," Madison keeps going. And going. "If you want my honest opinion, you're obviously too quiet to be much of a public speaker, so you'll need to speak clearly. Breathe through your stomach and don't stutter. Make sure your hair doesn't fall over your face; only well-groomed people are remembered. Also—"

Zack slides into the seat next to me. "Help," I whisper.

Unlike Madison, Zack has no problem hearing me. "If you're going to ask a question," he says, "it's pretty simple, right?"

"Excuse me," Madison says, glaring at Zack. "We were having a conversation."

"I thought you needed at least two people for that," Zack says, sounding surprised. "Wow, I'm learning a lot today."

Madison puffs out his cheeks. "Alan does not need your help. He's in good hands."

"I think Alan should be himself," Zack says.

Madison flaps his paper, diagrams and charts and all, toward Zack, waving it in front of my face. "It's much more complicated than that! There are laws and rules and when Alan asks his question—"

"I *can't do this*," I groan. It's so loud in here. Why is everything so loud?

Zack ruffles my hair, which I'm pretty sure nobody has done to me, ever. "Just be yourself," he says.

Before Madison can raise another objection, Principal Dorset calls for attention, and the crowd hushes. "Thank you, Evergreen," he says in his deep, baritone voice. "Today we are engaging in an important part of the democratic process. We will hold three debates here today for each grade's class president. They will take questions from you, after which you will cast your vote for one of them. I want to remind everyone—"

"Go Bridget!" yells someone from the front of the auditorium, followed by scattered clapping. Bridget waves and smiles. Talia grips the side of her podium.

"I want to *remind everyone*," Principal Dorset continues, "that you are middle schoolers; we expect you to act like them." He adjusts his tie. "The Sapling candidates have prepared opening statements. Miss MacDonald, you may go first."

Talia adjusts her microphone. She looks down at her podium—and says nothing.

Someone coughs.

"When I am class president," Talia starts, talking very slowly, "I am going to change some things. This will be, um, a school of competition and accountability and promise and, and, and—"

She drops her opening statement on the stage. Her hands are shaking, and her face is pale, and all her careful acts of confidence have fled out the fire exit. Talia's doing about as well as I would up there, which is really not what I want to be thinking about right now. A few people in the audience laugh as she scrambles to her feet, adjusting her glasses. "Um, that's all," she says quietly. "I'm done."

Principal Dorset says something to Talia away from his mic, but she just shakes her head. "Very well," the principal says. "Miss Harvey?"

"Thank you, Principal Dorset," Bridget says, flashing a perfectly white smile. "Being class president is such an important job, and I feel I am the best candidate possible. If elected, I will work to bring students and teachers together, and I will really listen to students' needs and do my best to serve the class and the school. Thank you very much."

More clapping, mostly from the front. "She didn't say anything!" Madison whispers. "She made a bunch of statements without any examples."

"Better than Talia," Rudy says from Madison's other side. "Yikes."

Miss Richter, standing to the side, shushes them.

Bridget smooths out her skirt and looks out into the audience, ready for the first question. Talia, however, keeps her eyes locked on her podium, chewing on her lip like her teeth are waging war against the rest of her face.

This is going to be a slaughter.

Sure enough, when someone asks the question of what the girls' favorite school subject is (which doesn't really seem relevant in a debate, as Madison is quick to grumble about), Bridget chimes in with, "Science and social studies, but I think every class has something to teach." Talia stammers out, "I—I like school." More people laugh this time.

After the third question—"Who's your favorite band?"—Principal Dorset says, "Remember: this is your chance to ask important questions, to choose the candidate that best represents you." That makes Madison poke my arm. I look down at the floor. There's got to be another way I can become well-known. There's got to be another way I can win the game.

I look up, and Zack is looking at me, smiling.

I hear Connor in my head talking about *the great Alan Cole.*

I see faces, faces everywhere. One of them could transform into my cretpoj. But my brother will never let me change the world if I don't stand up to him. It'll just keep happening, over and over, until there's no art left inside me. It won't ever stop unless I make it stop.

Dang it.

My hand trembles so much I can barely raise it. But I do.

And somewhere in this vast auditorium, right now, I

know Nathan's not bored anymore.

All eyes in the auditorium—every single kid at Evergreen—are on me now. The back of my shirt instantly gets wet. Someone passes the microphone to me. "Stand up," a kid a few rows in front of me calls, so I slowly get to my feet. It sure is bright when you stand up in the auditorium. Bright and blurry and, oh God, I think I'm going to faint.

"Do you have a question, young man?" Principal Dorset asks.

Of course I have a question! Why would I take the mic if I didn't have a question? But because I am a gigantic moron with a brain the size of a snowflake, I don't actually have a question. I was too busy being lulled by Zack's stupid encouragement, and I didn't bother to come up with one. Clearly this is his fault and not mine. I try to express all of this into the mic, to apologize up and down to the entire school for wasting their time and could they please let me use the little boys' room, I think I'm having bladder spasms, and my goodness those lights are bright, how can anyone see with those turned on full blast like that, I guess that's my question, hahaha thanks for letting me share this special time with you, but instead all that comes out of my mouth is, "Bruhgurglefoopfoopfranglepan."

"Young man, please ask a question or surrender the

mic," Principal Dorset says. "This debate is a serious process—"

Now, I don't know why it happens. I don't know what triggers it. I don't know if I'm tackling a serious issue or being myself or spewing out word vomit like I've got a vocabulary infection. Whatever the reason, I interrupt Principal Dorset, and I ask: "Where do babies come from?"

The entire auditorium—no, the entire *world*—starts howling with laughter. It's still not sinking in what I've asked, what I've done, until Madison practically shoves me back into my seat, and between the rippling, roaring waves of laughter from the entire school, I turn to fire and melt into a pool of ash on the floor.

That probably could've gone a little better.

"Everyone, quiet down!" Principal Dorset yells over the noise. "This is simply unacceptable behavior—you need to be quiet—"

"Alan," Zack yells, "Alan, look!"

I can barely raise my head, but I do anyway: Talia has taken the mic, determination carved into her cheeks. "It's simple," she says.

Then she starts to describe how babies are made.

In detail.

She doesn't get very far before she's drowned out by even *louder* laughter, and by Principal Dorset yanking the mic from her grip. She looks more surprised than embarrassed. (Bridget Harvey, by the way, is laughing along with everyone else.)

Principal Dorset barks into the mic, "Sapling teachers, please take your classes to homeroom. Your debate is over."

"What was that?" Madison groans as everyone files up to leave. "What *was* that? Alan—*what* was *that*?"

"I knew my fortune would come in handy," Zack says with a wide grin. "Didn't it, Alan? Didn't it predict your future?"

I can't speak. I can barely move. This was a train wreck of colossal proportions. It can't get any worse.

"Alan Cole!" Principal Dorset says into the mic, before we exit the auditorium. "Alan Cole! Stay here. You're coming with me."

Madison and Zack, finally united, both give me looks of horror. "Remember me as a hero," I croak as I make my way down the row, past all the kids who are—

Who are clapping me on the back.

Who are yelling, "Way to go, Alan!"

Huh.

. . . huh.

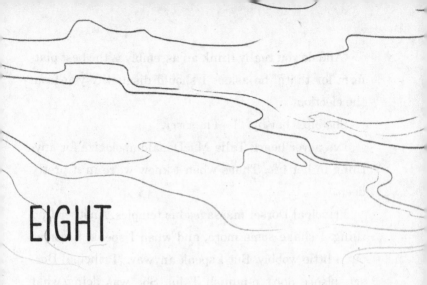

EIGHT

"—no idea about public decency. I could have angry letters from every parent of every child in this school because of—of—well, I don't have to repeat what you said, now do I?"

One month into middle school, and I'm already being yelled at by the principal, who, for the record, does not even let me get one word in when he marches me into his office. He's pretty angry. Not, like, Dad levels of angry, but still angry enough to give me the shakes. Then again, wouldn't you shake too, if you did what I did?

He doesn't go any easier on Talia, who gets shuffled into the office right next to me. "And to think," Principal Dorset continues, "a class president candidate spreading lewdness. In front of the entire student body!"

"I was saying the truth," Talia says.

"And do you really think an assembly is the best platform for that?" he asks. "I should disqualify you from the election."

She bites her lip. "I—I'm sorry."

I've never heard Talia MacDonald apologize for anything in her life. That's when I know we're in it pretty deep.

Principal Dorset massages his temples. Another Dad thing. I shake some more, and when I speak, it comes out a little wobbly. But I speak anyway. "Principal Dorset, please don't p-punish Talia. She was doing what you're s-supposed to do at debates."

"What you're supposed to do?" Principal Dorset asks. "Young man, don't you understand we can't talk about these topics whenever we please? There are rules, and you've broken them."

"She was doing what she had to. If you were up in front of all those kids, and—and people were laughing at you because you dropped your paper, and you wanted really badly to win the election and you cared so much that all you wanted was for somebody to ask you a question, just so you could answer it and show everybody how smart you were, wouldn't you, um—wouldn't you . . ." I lose the words, and I look down at the floor.

There's a silence in Principal Dorset's office. No ticking clock like at home. Just the distant hum of an air conditioner. Then a thought slaps me across the heart like an electric shock: Principal Dorset could call Dad over this. I grip the edges of the chair. Maybe if I hold on tight enough, I won't ever have to go home.

Finally, the principal speaks. "Young lady, what you did was inappropriate, and you must be punished for it. However, I will not disqualify you from the election."

Talia squeezes the bottom of her chair. I can practically hear her swallow. "Thank you," she squeaks.

"But you both must be punished," Principal Dorset continues. "I think a detention for each of you will do. That should give you plenty of time to think about what you've done."

He dismisses us without calling home. I stop holding my breath. I didn't even realize I was holding my breath, but I was.

Neither of us talks in the hall. Talia doesn't even look at me. When I finally get up the nerve to say something, even though I don't know what it is (you'd think I would've learned my lesson), she walks away to her next class and leaves me behind.

She's going to lose the election, and it'll all be my fault. Maybe I should've let her get disqualified instead.

Well, it's not like she would've won anyway.

That makes me feel a little better, at least. But only a little.

The weirdest things are always the things you don't expect to happen. If it rained turnips and oysters one day, that'd be pretty weird, because it's unexpected. If your fingers spontaneously turned into mini garden hoses that spurted out lighter fluid, yeah, weird, yeah, unexpected.

When I walk in to my third period class to spontaneous applause, that's unexpected.

When I walk down the hall and kids yell things like, "There he is!" "Great question, Cole!" and "Best part of that assembly!"

When even the older kids start looking at me with smiles—and they're not mean smiles.

When I'm treated like a celebrity by kids I've known since first grade but who've never said one word to me.

And the other kids, who come from other elementary schools, know my name, because Principal Dorset called it out at the end of the assembly. Everyone knows who I am.

That's unexpected.

What's even more unexpected than all of this, as if anything could be more unexpected than a popular ninth grader high-fiving me in the bathroom, is when

I'm on my way to the cafeteria, and a hand reaches out and drags me into the same empty classroom as a few days ago.

"Al."

Nathan doesn't look too good. Marcellus, right next to him, crosses his arms. "What's going on, goldfish?" my brother asks. "I didn't think you had it in you."

I don't say anything.

"And you said I was the weird one in the family," Nathan says to Marcellus.

Marcellus nods. "You are."

Nathan holds up his hands. "I might be a little weird, but I'd never do what Al did. You seriously asked 'Where do babies come from?' in front of the whole school?"

I nod.

Nathan inhales. "Why?"

I pause. "I want to win."

Marcellus whispers something into Nathan's ear. Something that sounds an awful lot like "Told you."

Like he's a piñata I broke in half, Nathan opens his mouth a few times, but no words come out. Finally he shakes his head. "Enjoy it," he spits. "Won't last long."

He shoves me out of the way with his shoulder, mutters "Come on" to Marcellus, and leaves the empty room. Marcellus looks back at me for a few moments, then he follows. And they're gone.

Did you ever experience a new emotion? Like bits of your body start to stir like a vat full of magic potion, and what bubbles up is a totally new experience. Like when I breathe, there's less stuff tethering me down. Like my eyes can focus on what's directly in front of me and not have to scan sideways, just to make sure nothing sneaks up on me. Like my heart beats a little clearer with every step I take toward the cafeteria, like my legs make longer strides on the linoleum.

Two down, five to go.

Now that's unexpected.

I wait in the lunch line, hungry yet again, when this horrible dying-lizard-in-heat sound penetrates my ear. "Hi, Zack," I say without turning around.

"Dang," Zack says. "Guess that only works once, huh?"

"Guess so." We move up in line.

Zack smiles. "Looks like everyone's talking about you. What kind of punishment did you get?"

"A detention."

"Wow. It could be worse. They could've shot you out of a cannon."

I hold my tray out to get food. "Yeah, that would've been worse."

Zack thanks the lunch lady, then says, "I hope Talia wins."

A little twinge disrupts my good feelings. "Me too."

Before we get to the Unstable Table (but after we pass a group of kids wondering about the vending machine outside Miss Richter's room), someone calls, "Alan! Hey, Alan!" I look to the voice and—oh my God—it's Connor, sitting at the table next to ours, and he's motioning me over, pointing to an empty seat next to his.

I stop walking completely, and Zack promptly crashes into my back, almost sending our food all over the place.

Connor Garcia wants me to—wants *me* to—

I can see Madison watching us from the Unstable Table, eating from his bagged lunch. I take a deep breath, mumble "Sorry" to Zack, and head toward the seat next to Connor, trying not to look back at my former tablemates. It isn't until I get to Connor's table that my gut does a backflip and I start wondering if I'm going to be able to keep my food down.

And I thought the debate was bad.

"Hey, man," Connor says with a big smile, one that's directed squarely at *me*. "That was really awesome today. Guys, this is Alan, he's in my ASPEN classes. He's really cool."

He's really cool.

"What were you thinking today?" Connor asks. "Why'd you ask that?"

When the guy you like invites you to sit at his lunch

table of popular kids and actually takes an interest in something you did—something *you did*—and asks why you did it, it helps to come up with a good answer. Something to make you seem really interesting and amazing and maybe even worthy enough to *like*. Naturally, all I can do is sputter, "It was funny—I mean, I guess. Funny. It was. Uh, pretty funny. Babies. I mean, babies. Funny. Yes."

Connor doesn't say anything for what feels like eighteen hours, then he half shrugs and goes back to eating.

I'll take it.

The four other kids at Connor's table—the Stable Table, I guess—don't seem too interested in me. They start talking about soccer, and how both the boys' and girls' teams are going to slaughter Broadleaf Middle School next week. (I've learned over the past month that I'm supposed to hate Broadleaf. I don't have anything against the school, until Connor calls them punks at the table, and then I despise them with all my might.) Then Connor asks me, "How'd you do on the English homework, Alan?"

"Uh," I say, very aware of all these big tough jocks looking at me. "I did okay, I guess."

Connor shakes his head. "I can't keep all this simple, compound, complex clause stuff straight. I don't know how you do it."

"Hey, he's a nerd," one familiar-looking guy at the Stable Table says. "Nerd brains are like mini computers."

I frown, but this guy doesn't look away from me, and eventually my eyes drop to my lunch tray.

"Come on, Ron," Connor says.

Ron raises his arms. "Just joking around. Besides, it's true."

"Ron doesn't like it when people are better at things than he is," Connor whispers to me, but not so quiet the rest of the table can't hear. "He's never happy."

Ron tosses a ketchup packet at Connor, who laughs. I glance over at the Unstable Table. Looks like Zack is going on and on about something, and Madison is quietly eating his salad, probably doing his best to ignore Zack. I catch Madison look up at me once, and his eyes instantly drop back down. My stomach gurgles.

"So what's your deal anyway?" Ron asks through a mouthful of french fries.

It takes me a second to realize he's talking to me. "What do you mean?" I ask.

"Why don't you know how to swim?"

Then I realize where I've seen Ron before: he's in my swimming class. "I, uh, never learned."

"It's not that hard," Ron says. "Every time I see you in class, you're just splashing around. Looks like you're not even trying."

Connor pipes up, "Ron, come on, man."

Ron raises a hand. "I'm just saying. Don't they have pools in Dorktopia?"

Snickers from around the table. "I wouldn't know," I say with as much bite as I can muster, because I am an idiot.

Ron continues, "Didn't your dad ever teach you? My dad taught me when I was two."

In my head I can hear Dad grumbling about how *I don't have time to teach you* and *we're never going to the ocean anyway, so why even bother?* Those were the only reasons he gave to me and Nathan.

"Some people are scared of the water," says a girl I recognize from Pine Garden.

Ron shrugs. "Some people are pussies."

I can feel my face flush. This is not turning out the way I wanted it to. I look over to the Unstable Table again, and Zack is pretending to be an airplane, complete with arm movements and loud sound effects. Madison is staring off into space.

Eventually the conversation shifts away from me, and the other kids talk about other things. Connor taps me on the arm while I sit in silence. "Sorry," he whispers. "Ron can be a jerk sometimes."

"It's fine," I lie. I hope he doesn't notice my goose bumps.

Connor motions toward the Unstable Table, where Zack is pointing at me and waving me over. "I think you're being paged," Connor says.

I stand up. The rest of the Stable Table doesn't even notice.

"Hey," Connor says before I leave. "I don't care what Ron says. I think you're awesome." He lightly punches me on the arm.

I float back to the Unstable Table, barely aware of my feet on the floor. "Hey," Zack says from a quadrillion miles away, "I was telling a great joke and I thought you should hear it."

"Well," huffs a Madison-shaped cloud, "I guess you're not quite so cool that you can't sit with us anymore."

Zack watches me. "You look different."

That reaches me. "Huh?"

"You're smiling," he says.

I move my mouth a little. Sure enough, my lips are curved up. I'm smiling.

I'm smiling.

Madison doesn't seem to notice. He grumbles, "Today I'm going to my family's health club. That's going to be unpleasant. There'll be lots of running and swimming and possibly protein shakes, and none of that sounds fun at all."

"Hang on," I say. "Swimming?"

"Yes," Madison continues. "There's a pool. I like to swim, but after already doing it during school I'd rather not."

The gears in my brain turn fast. "Do you still want me to be your pupil?"

Madison leans into the Unstable Table. "Go on."

The school week is almost over. Two days into CvC and I've somehow set plenty of things spinning into motion: hidden papers, lucky underwear, rapid ascents to popularity, and even a "fitness consultation" (in his words) this weekend with Madison, at this private health club. He was practically giddy about it. He can't be a worse swimming instructor than Marcellus, right?

We're about to leave ASPEN English class, the last class of the day, when Principal Dorset comes on the loudspeaker. "I would like to announce the results of our class president elections."

In the front row, Talia hunches over.

"The Shrub class president is Kelly Richards."

Clapping and cheering from down the hall.

"The Sprout class president is Darnell Simmons."

Talia rolls her pencil back and forth between her fingers so hard they almost catch fire.

"And the Sapling class president is"—long pause—"Talia MacDonald."

A loud gasp comes out of Talia's mouth, and she practically slumps over in her desk. Mrs. Ront, our English teacher, leads us in applause.

Principal Dorset continues, "Congratulations to our winners, and to our runners-up for trying their best. All class presidents should report to my office first thing Monday morning."

I tune out the loudspeaker and stare at Talia instead. She looks stunned. More than stunned—like this outcome was so far removed from possibility, it broke her brain a little. Like she'd given up.

People congratulate Talia as they leave the room (Rudy says, "How could I not vote for you after that answer?"). But our class president only wants to talk to one person, and she makes her way to my desk. "Alan Cole," she says.

"Hi," I say.

"I won."

I nod.

She breaks the stare. "I would have . . . not won, if you hadn't asked your question."

"That's not—"

"Don't patronize me. I stunk up the auditorium like bad gym socks. I'm not . . . all that good with big crowds. But I told myself I was going to answer the next question truthfully, no matter what it was. I blanked out, and I went for it, and—and that's why I won. No other reason."

Talia adjusts her glasses. "Of course, this creates a problem for us."

Uh-oh. "A problem?"

"I owe you," she says. "I'm in your debt. Not just from the debate, but also from when we were in the office. I would've been disqualified if not for you. I owe you a favor, so tell me what you want soon, so it can stop hanging over my head."

"You don't have to—"

"Don't be ridiculous. I always pay back my debts. That doesn't mean I enjoy doing it, though. Think it over."

She turns to leave the room, but stops. "It's not easy for me to admit when I . . ." She trails off. "Thanks."

Unexpected things can be good or bad. But sometimes getting something good *at all* is unexpected, whether it's becoming the most well-known kid in school, or winning a class election, or getting to teach someone something you're good at. Or getting called awesome and cool by your crush.

Sometimes, when it seems like the whole world is against you, something unexpected—something good—can happen. Maybe it's those moments that make everything else seem less bad. Maybe it's those moments that make you smile.

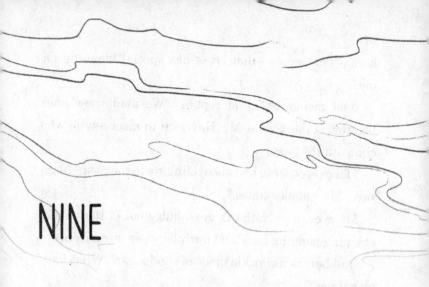

NINE

"Tomorrow's the company dinner," Dad says. "Hannah Jackson's kid won the county spelling bee."

Before Dad even finishes speaking, Nathan bursts out, "*Ursprache.* U-R-S-P-R-A-C-H-E. A hypothetically reconstructed parent language. *Balalaika.* B-A-L-A-L-A-I-K-A. A Russian stringed musical instrument. *Psittacine.* P-S-I-T-T-A-C-I-N-E. Of or relating to parrots. I can keep going."

(He could. And has.)

"You've got your best jewelry?" Dad asks Mom.

Mom nods. "I have Mommy's cross."

"Your mother's jewelry?" Dad shakes his head. "You should wear the one I bought for you."

Mom doesn't look at her plate this time. Instead she

says, "That cross—that cross has special meaning for me."

"Old memories," Dad replies. "We made new ones together. I don't want Mr. Harrison to meet a wife who clings to the past."

"There's nothing bad about clinging to the past," Mom says. "To happier times."

My eyes, and Nathan's eyes, bulge out of their sockets, ping-ponging back and forth between our parents.

Dad laughs a chuckle made of sandpaper. "What happier times?"

Mom looks down.

"Be happy now," Dad says. "Happy for my promotion. Wear my cross and don't disappoint me."

Mom wrings her hands but says nothing.

Dad massages his temples and looks at me. "What sports do you play?"

It takes me a few seconds to find my voice. "I run long distance, I play shortstop, and I'd show you my bicycle kick if I remembered to bring my soccer ball."

Dad raises his eyebrows. "No mistakes. You've been practicing. Good job."

His praise reaches me, but it doesn't have the same effect it usually does. I look down at my plate.

"Dad," Nathan says. If words could tiptoe, he'd be creeping around a corner. "Can't I go over to Marcellus's? You don't need me there."

"Everybody's going," Dad says.

"But Dad—"

Dad raises his head. "You have one job tomorrow. This isn't one of your history tests, little pig, so don't make any mistakes. Be like your brother."

It's like Dad slaps Nathan across the face. Dad stands up, which is the cue that dinner's over, so Nathan immediately runs upstairs. Mom slowly clears the table, balancing four plates. She drops a knife. I look around—no Dad.

When Mom reaches the sink, I tap her on the shoulder and hold out the knife. She takes the utensil from me and turns back around.

I grab a dish towel and start drying the dishes she washes. She watches me as she hands me a plate, a little smile on her face. I almost give her a smile back, but then—

"What are you doing?"

Dad appears from behind me. I look between my parents as I absentmindedly dry the same spot on the wet plate.

"Leave it," Dad says. "If you want to be useful, help me in the garage. This is your mother's job."

"I was just helping," I squeak out.

"This is your mother's job."

He watches me—they both watch me. Slowly, looking down, I place the rag and the plate on the counter and walk upstairs. I can't look her in the eyes.

The awesome and cool Alan Cole, who's completed two out of seven CvC tasks, who's currently the most well-known kid in school, can't even help his mom with the dishes.

What a coward I am.

But now, as I walk into my room and stare out at Big Green, it's officially the weekend, and even though that awful party lingers in the background like somebody's bad cologne, I can finally relax. I can start my cretpoj, because now I know who it's going to be a portrait of, and I make for my art supplies—

—until I'm tackled to the floor, tasting a face full of carpet.

"Mmrph!" I try to spit, but he presses my face down hard with one hand, and with the other hand he takes my left arm and holds it out behind my back, at just the right angle where I know, if he twists it the right way, it'll snap off.

With his knee he digs into my back. My vision's getting white; little discs of light swim in my eyes. He yanks on my arm and I scream, muffled by the rug.

Everything is spinning and I think I'm going to throw up dinner, and he pulls my arm up and away from my body, and I hear this terrible cracking noise, and I think, oh my God, he broke it, and there's a little voice inside me that says, *at least now you won't have to go to the company dinner*, but that voice goes away with one final yank. I scream again, and now I'm breathing really heavy, and I'm sobbing like a little baby.

He reduced me to this in under a minute.

He hops off me and spins me around onto my back. I can't even sit up, I'm so dizzy. I rub my arm. Still in one piece. Looks like I'm going to the dinner after all.

Nathan snarls, "You think you're smarter than me, huh?"

My head's still swimming; what he's saying isn't sinking in.

He slaps me—hard—on the cheek. "You do. You think you're smarter than me. You little piece of crap."

I'm still crying a little, trying to regain my breath, my footing. "Nathan—"

He drags me to my feet and presses me against the wall, right underneath my poster of *The Old Guitarist*. "Say it," he spits in my face. "Say I'm smarter than you."

"You're—hic—smarter than me."

"Louder!"

"You're smarter than me. You're smarter—hic—th-than me."

Nathan's eyes narrow, and he lets me go. I massage

my tingly arm and rub my cheek, finally almost catching my breath. My brother paces around my room, angrier than I've seen him in a long time. "I found it," he finally says.

I keep quiet. This is one of those times where it's best to sit, and watch, and brace myself for the next wave.

Nathan pulls something out of his pocket and tosses it onto my bed: a small, folded-up piece of paper that says *NATHAN* on it. "Band room," he says. "Did you really think I wouldn't look there? I know how you think, because you're dumber than me."

"Oh," I squeak.

"And I made someone cry," he goes on. "That's two for me. We're tied."

I almost ask who. Then I hiccup. Right.

Nathan continues, "I joined the swim team today. Not enough people signed up over the summer, so they took me on. I'll learn to swim by Thursday. You'll never get that paper out of the vending machine, or do anything else. You're going down, goldfish. And when you do, I'll make sure to let everybody know your terrible little secret."

And it finally occurs to me, where all this is coming from.

I've seen Nathan scared plenty of times before, but all of them were a result of Dad.

This is the first time he's ever been scared of me.

Nathan starts to laugh. Not his hyena's cackle, loud and brash—this is uneven, spastic, frantic. "I'm going to have fun destroying you," he growls. "You're a disgrace. You're barely even human. Soon I'll make you pay for even thinking you could be smarter than me."

He stomps out of my room and slams the door shut, leaving me rubbing my arm and wiping my eyes.

Why did I think, even for a second, this was possible?

I wish I knew what was making him freak out like this, why he suddenly thinks I'm a threat. When he beats me up he normally enjoys it, but this wasn't enjoyment. I don't even know what it was. He's never felt threatened by me in a CvC game before. Is it the unbelievable idea he might not win something? Or is it something else?

A low vibrating hum snaps me back to my room: my phone's going off from a text. There are only two non-family people who have my number, and both of them got it after lunch today. Sure enough, the text message reads:

What time should I pick you up tomorrow?

I inch into my chair, still tender all over. My old sketchbook sits on my desk. The tingling in my body fades as I reach for the last empty page and my paints.

But first, I type my response:

earlier the better.

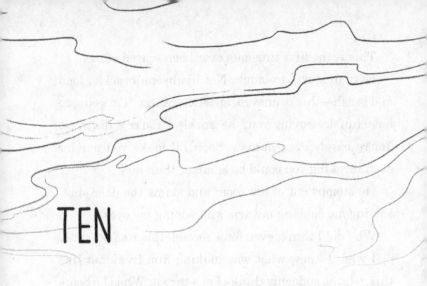

TEN

The Trumans pull up to 16 Werther Street on Saturday morning. One chipper knock on the door and I'm running down with a backpack crammed with a bathing suit, a towel, and some money and snacks. I forgot to ask Madison how much this fancy-pants health club costs to get in, so I brought eight bucks and twenty-two cents. I had significantly more than eight bucks and twenty-two cents to my name a few days ago, when a certain big brother swiped a certain little brother's funds. Hopefully eight bucks and twenty-two cents won't just get me one lap around the pool and some protein powder to sip through a straw.

I run downstairs with more energy than usual. Partly because I'm eager to get out of the house. But also partly because somebody started his cretpoj last night, and somebody's a little jazzed about it.

I don't care what anyone says. I think you're awesome.

By the time I reach the door, Dad's gotten there first.

"Hello, sir," Madison says, standing perfectly straight. He extends his hand. "My name is Madison Wilson Truman. I'm Alan's coach. I'm here to pick him up for his fitness consultation."

Dad stands there, completely still. I guess Madison realizes his handshake is fizzling like a busted firework, so he drops his hand clumsily to his side and says, "This really is a lovely home you have here. Such nice carpeting. Green carpet—who would've guessed?"

I walk closer to the door before this can get any worse. "Hey. I'm ready."

My presence seems to spur Dad back into motion. He says, "My son didn't tell me he made plans. I thought for sure he'd remember the important dinner he's going to tonight." The voice is light, but there's nothing light about the words.

The back of my shirt gets wet. "I'll be back by five."

"Of course you will," Dad says. "At four thirty."

I nod.

Dad smiles at Madison. "If you don't bring him back by then, you can cook him for dinner." He laughs once, then twice, each time sounding like a hawk swooping down to catch its favorite meal.

I can hardly shut the door fast enough.

As we walk outside, Madison mutters, "Er, your father is very—"

"You don't have to," I say.

Madison exhales. "Okay. I won't."

"Sorry about that," I say. "I wouldn't make a very good dinner anyway."

"You're right," Madison says as we arrive at the tiny car parked at the curb. "You're probably better with breakfast."

He laughs, and I laugh a little too, and the autumn wind whips past my hair and gets in my eyes. Big Green waves good-bye as I climb into the car.

The woman in the driver's seat smiles. "You must be Alan. I'm Dorothy Truman. This is my husband, Bob."

"How're you doing, champ?" Bob Truman reaches across the backseat and shakes my hand.

"Hi," I say. "Thanks for letting me use your club."

"It's not *our* club, champ," Mr. Bob Truman says as Mrs. Dorothy Truman pulls out of the driveway. "Helen's Crest Health and Fitness Club belongs to all its members. As of today, you're a member."

"I, uh," I say, turning red, "I don't have a lot of money—"

Dorothy Truman squeezes the brakes in the middle of Werther Street, sending me lurching forward. "Maddie! Did you tell your friend he had to pay?"

"Er, no, not quite," Madison stammers. "I just didn't mention it—"

"Maddie," Bob Truman says, speaking very slowly. "This is what we keep talking about. Acting like a grown-up. You don't act like a grown-up when you lie to your friends. Isn't that right?"

"But I wasn't—"

"If you want us to treat you like a grown-up," Dorothy Truman says, "you need to act like one. Isn't that right?"

Madison slumps in the seat. "Yes, ma'am," he grumbles.

I can practically see the little thought bubble above Madison's head: *Alan, back me up.*

We spend some time in the car quietly brainstorming ways to break into an empty vending machine, but when Bob Truman says we should speak up and share with the rest of the car, we clam up pretty fast.

When we arrive at Helen's Crest, Dorothy Truman says we're free to explore, but not to use any equipment without adult supervision. (Madison sighs softly when she says that.)

"Whoa," I say once we walk in. This place is out of control. Flat-screen TVs on every corner, shiny exercise equipment, older boys drinking smoothies . . . something about that last image is really appealing, and it isn't the berry protein blast. All of a sudden I'm very aware of where my eyes are looking, so I find a nonmuscular spot on the wall to stare at for a bit.

Madison's mom stops at the women's locker room. "Remember, Maddie: fifteen pounds by the end of the month. You want the girls to like you, not laugh at you, right?"

"Yes, ma'am," Madison mumbles. He shuffles into the men's locker room.

When I make for the water fountain, Bob Truman stops me. "Thank you, Adam," he says.

"Um, it's Alan," I say, wiping my mouth. "For what?"

Madison's dad smiles. "Our boy isn't the best at making friends. We've tried to get him to tone it down, but he isn't learning. It's nice to know someone feels bad enough for him to give him a chance."

I can feel my face flush. "I don't feel bad for Madison. He's teaching me to swim."

Bob Truman laughs, then stops laughing when I don't join in. "You're serious?" he asks. "He's teaching you?"

I swallow. "Mr. Truman—"

"It's Bob, Adam."

"—Madison doesn't, uh, need my pity. He's, um, he's fine the way he is. Maybe you, maybe—maybe you could—"

Mr. Truman claps me on the back. "You're a real good

kid, Adam. Real good kid." He lets the word *kid* linger a little, smiles, and heads into the locker room.

The guy in my cretpoj told me I was awesome. How awesome can I be if I can't stand up for anyone?

Madison changes into a bathing suit but also wears a baggy T-shirt that says "I <3 My Library," and he doesn't get in the pool with me. Instead he hovers at the water's edge, feet dangling into the blue-green liquid. "Very well," he commands, his voice echoing in the almost empty pool. "Let us begin."

"You're not getting in?" I ask. My voice barely registers through the sounds of middle-aged women splashing nearby.

"I'd rather not," he says. "If you want my honest opinion, I can advise you better from up here."

Thirty seconds in and he's about on the level of Marcellus. Surely a promising sign of things to come.

I grab on to the wall of the pool with both hands and get ready, because what else am I going to do? The pool here is even bigger than Evergreen's, and the water seems cleaner too. A lifeguard sits at the reverse end of the pool, flipping through a magazine, and those women Mom's age are doing laps on the other side, so I've got plenty of space to practice.

Madison clears his throat. "This is my promise to

you: I, Madison Wilson Truman, will teach you to swim by—what's the deadline for your game again?"

"Friday morning."

Another throat-clearing, this one a lot quieter. "Right. How much do you know again?"

"I know how to circle one leg at a time."

Madison puffs out his cheeks. "Right. Okay. Right. By Friday, you say?"

"This isn't very encouraging," I say.

Madison scoffs, "There's no time to waste on encouragement. I've outlined a comprehensive program guaranteed to get results. That's the Truman Doctrine." He chuckles.

I look out at the vast stretch of water that is the Helen's Crest Health and Fitness Club pool, and my stomach gets that funny feeling, like my small intestine's being tied up like a pair of shoelaces.

"First item on the program," Madison goes on, ticking items off on his fingers. "You're going to swim from the deep end of the pool to the shallow end, then back again to the deep end in one trip. This builds character. It will make you stronger and more comfortable in the water. We'll do that a few times, then you'll do it with your eyes closed to really learn to sense the water around you."

The echoes of Madison's voice and the splashes of the

water fade, and they're replaced with things like:

So what's your deal anyway? Why don't you know how to swim? Some people are pussies.

And things like:

Soon I'll make you pay for even thinking you could be smarter than me.

And laughter. A hawk's laughter.

Then I look up at Madison, at his face (he's not even looking at me while he talks), and I think of how I would capture everything in those eyes. How he acts around his parents. What he thinks teaching me will actually prove. Why he doesn't want to take his shirt off, even when there's barely anybody around, and how he feels when he has to actually do it in school. He could be another cretpoj. Another painting to change the world. So much to paint, so much to capture.

So little time to make even one.

My fingers grip the wall tight, so tight they turn bright white.

"—then we'll get started on underwater weights, which are very—"

"Madison."

"—good at strength training your muscles, which, once you start taking cold showers, can really work on your stamina—"

"Madison."

He stops.

"Can I have a kickboard?" I ask.

"That's not part of the program," he says.

"But I want to learn to swim, not learn to drown." (I already know how to do that.) "And you need to get down here in the water with me."

Madison raises his head. "Excuse me? I'm your teacher and you're my student. I know what's best for you."

"This would make sure you get your exercise in too—"

"Oh?" Madison barks. The lifeguard turns her head. "Now you're being my parents? I want a student, not another family member who'll—" He squeezes his eyes shut.

"You don't have to help me as a teacher," I say quietly. "Help me as a friend."

Something shifts and changes on Madison's face, and even though his eyes are shut tight, his features twist, his nostrils expand, his mouth opens. A warmth spreads across my stomach, beats against my rib cage, bubbles into my face.

"Madison," I whisper. "Please."

He gets up and walks away. Sighing, I lift myself out of the pool, but then he comes back a few seconds later with a kickboard. He tugs his shirt over his head and, talking in a higher-pitched voice than usual, says, "Let's get started."

And thus begins my first lesson with Madison Wilson Truman, swimming instructor and . . . friend.

ELEVEN

"You're late," Dad says as I walk in the door at four fifteen. "Hurry up and get ready. We've got to be early, early, early."

I nod, heading upstairs, but then Dad stops me. "What's that smell?"

"Huh?"

He takes a big whiff of my damp hair. "Chlorine. Why do you smell like chlorine?"

"I, uh, went swimming. That's why."

"You went *swimming*?" Dad's voice gets thin. "No more swimming. It's bad enough you're doing it in school, but now you're doing it for fun too? No more swimming!"

"But Dad—"

He raises his head.

I look down at the floor and slowly march upstairs.

"Be ready in half an hour," he calls from downstairs.

Great. So now I'm banned from fitness consultations, with five days to go to pass the test. I really got a lot out of my time with Madison today too; once he got in the water with me, he actually showed me ways to stay afloat, and he helped me work on my kicking. When he said I'd basically need to come here and practice for hours every day, I said that was fine, and he said it was fine with him too.

Now I don't know what to do.

Changing into my suit—for *special* occasions—makes me realize I haven't given this dinner much thought, even though Dad's been harping on about it for months. What are we going to actually do there? Is Dad's boss going to make a speech? Will I be able to stay awake from all the adultspeak? Will they have lots of food? (I hope they have lots of food.)

Will I say the wrong thing and make Dad angry?

I report to the living room, all suited up and ready to go. Mom stands off to the side, running her fingers along the cross around her neck. Nathan fidgets—he hates getting dressed up. Dad walks in from the kitchen, and we line up for inspection.

He starts with Nathan, who stops fidgeting immediately and stands stiffly, barely even breathing. Then Dad walks to me, taking a big sniff of my hair. Apparently satisfied, he looks me up and down. "Nathan, fix your brother's tie."

Grumbling, my brother walks over and adjusts my tie, which I think might be the first time in my whole life he's actually touched me without leaving a bruise.

Dad moves over to Mom—and he freezes, staring at the cross around her neck. A cross that's definitely not the one Dad bought for her. He opens his mouth, but Mom's hand clasps the cross protectively. Nathan and I look at each other, disbelieving.

Finally, Dad massages his temples, swallows a big glass of water, and marches out the door. Mom closes her eyes and whispers something. A prayer? A thank-you?

I follow Dad, trying to ignore the warning pangs in my gut. I almost ask myself, *what's the worst that could really happen*, but I've read enough stories in twelve years to know people who ask that always wind up with their houses burning down or a passenger plane crashing on their big toes, so instead I ask myself, *what's the best that could really happen*, because, hey, reverse psychology is a thing, right?

Boy, I wish I was wearing Orville right about now.

Dad works for a place called Harrison Money Group (HMG), and they handle financial stuff all over Flower County. He specifically does behind-the-scenes number crunching; he doesn't normally interact with clients (which I'm sure isn't much of a shock to you). Growing up I always had this idea Dad worked in a windowless office full of people like him, who all went home and treated their families like he treated his. So I'm a little surprised when we pull up to the Flower County Community Center, and after one final "Don't disappoint me" from Dad, we're greeted by a smiling man yelling, "James!"

Dad always goes by James. Nobody dares to call him Jim, and especially not Jimmy. He pulls his lips back in something clearly meant to resemble a warm smile. "Hello, Richard," he says in a higher-pitched voice, which I guess is how he thinks nice people talk.

Richard shakes Dad's hand. "This is my little girl, Elizabeth," he says, gesturing to a girl a few years younger than me.

"Oh, is this the girl who plays the cello?" Dad asks, looking at Nathan.

Nathan clears his throat and says, "I was first chair last year in the Evergreen Middle School orchestra, and the orchestra is going to perform a piece I've written this year."

"Wow," Elizabeth says.

Richard laughs. "Well, that's quite the son you've got there, James. See you inside."

Dad places a hand on Nathan's shoulder. The presence of the hand is so startling that Nathan actually flinches, but Dad leaves it there long after Richard and his daughter have moved toward the main entrance. I guess Dad remembers he doesn't have to pretend to be nice around us, and he removes his hand and says, "Put more enthusiasm into it next time." But he still looks back at us a few times as we walk.

The main reception area of the community center is big, even though it feels smaller than the Helen's Crest pool. There are tables with nice tablecloths and silverware set up by a stage (great, so there *is* going to be a speech). Men in suits and women in dresses chitchat over drinks. A huge punch bowl decorates the middle of the food tables.

I *really* feel like I don't belong here. There's barely anyone my age. And there's all these people I've never met talking about things I don't know anything about. I wish I was back home in Dorktopia.

We take a seat near the front of the stage. Dad gets greeted by a few more people—"James!" "Hey, James!"—and Nathan and I say our lines like we practiced, sitting there like ugly props on a bad movie set. After I tell a smiling-too-hard woman about my bicycle kick, Dad whispers to me, "Much better than drawing. Nobody's impressed by artists." I turn red. A wide smirk fills Nathan's face. Mom looks at me, running her hands along her mother's cross; she gives me a small smile. I don't return it.

As I settle into my seat, a girl in the next chair over watches me. She isn't blinking. I look down at my empty plate.

Finally someone gets up to the podium. I guess this is Dad's boss, Mr. Harrison, who doesn't need to introduce himself and gives everyone a big hello and thanks for being at the first HMG company dinner (if this goes well, there will be more!) and thanks for another great fiscal year, and then he goes on about some of the great strides HMG has made in the past twelve months and oh hey something is brushing against my leg.

The girl next to me, who looks about my age, is watching the speech with her head in her hand, looking very much like she'd rather be eating a whole cactus than listening to Mr. Harrison talk about how the office "went green" this year by switching to double-sided printing. But even though she isn't looking at me, I can feel her foot poke my foot underneath the table.

This is new.

Dad is listening to the speech, clapping at all the right parts; Mom is smiling faintly, cupping her cross in her hands; and Nathan is trying to organize his silverware in fun shapes. No one's watching. I gulp. Then, slowly, before my brain catches up with the rest of me, I nudge her leg with my foot.

The girl doesn't make any visible change, but as I pull my foot away, she taps my leg with her foot. The second time I poke her, it's a little less terrifying, but then she stops. No acknowledgment of my desire to continue the game. I can't see her face over her hand from this angle. I ignore the little pang of curious disappointment in my chest and try to focus on the speech. After I zone out again, something touches my arm—there's a little piece of paper there. Again checking to see if anyone's watching me, I unfold it. It says:

Mr. Harrison has a booger in his nose.

I look at the stage. I'm close enough that I can see him, and yeah, he's got a little green lump dangling from his right nostril. A snicker escapes my lips, which makes Dad look over at me. I shove the piece of paper in my pocket before he notices.

After approximately three years, Mr. Harrison ends his speech to applause. He invites everyone to eat, and then he starts making the rounds at all the tables. Fortunately, he doesn't start with ours. I've had enough Mr. Harrison for five company dinners.

Dad maneuvers Mom over to another table with something probably meant to be friendliness, and Nathan escapes to a corner so he can text Marcellus about what a horrible evening he's having, so it's just me and this girl at the table. Finally turning to face me, she asks, "Do you want to be an accountant like your dad?"

"I don't want to be anything like my dad," I say.

It takes me a second to realize what I said. To a total stranger. "S-Sorry," I stammer.

The girl studies me like she's a microscope on a microbe, pushing her eyebrows together. "Why are you sorry? I don't care if you hate your dad."

"I don't *hate* my dad," I say. Every other Cole in the room is out of earshot, thank God. Then, to change the subject, I say, "Where are your parents?"

"Around," the girl says. "Are you hungry?"

I nod.

She stands up, looks around the main room, returns her sharp eyes back to me, nods, and marches off, all in the span of about three seconds. "For the record," she says as we walk toward the buffet line, "I'm impressed by artists."

I turn bright red.

"What's your pleasure?" she asks, scooping a generous helping of pasta onto her plate.

"Huh?"

"Your art. What do you do?"

Too many people are jostling around the buffet line, and Dad's a few feet down, so I whisper, "I paint."

She nods. "Artists understand things other people don't. People like your dad."

I don't say anything. I'm too busy watching my traveling companion take huge helpings of everything on the buffet line, despite being about as skinny as me. Everything except the salad, which she totally skips.

As we return to our table, the girl asks, "You don't say much, do you?"

I shrug.

She smiles. "That's fine. People who talk too much don't listen. I'm sure you impress all the girls with your great listening skills."

I look down. "Right."

"Anyway," she says through a mouthful of scalloped potatoes, "if I'm nice to you, will you hook me up with your brother? He's really hot."

A little pasta gets lodged in my throat in a sort of half snort. "Don't worry. He's single."

"I could only hope so," she says. "Swoooooooon." She pretends to fan herself.

"My name's Alan," I say.

"Names? On the first date? Names are meaningless, Pedro. But if you want, you can call me June."

"I think I will."

"Ho ho! Alan and June, together at last! This calls for a celebration. Do you like red or white wine?"

"I wouldn't know," I say.

"Punch it is." She lifts her glass into the air. "To art."

I laugh a little. "To art."

Our glasses clink together in a toast and we take great big sips. The chilled, sugary liquid flows through me with a jolt of energy, the sweetness lingers in my throat, and I smile. So does she. "Alan," she says, rolling my name on her tongue. "Do you go to Broadleaf? I haven't seen you there."

Uh-oh. I'm now supposed to hate her guts and boo her teams at sporting events. Hope the Stable Table doesn't catch wind of this. "I go to Evergreen. I'm in seventh grade."

"So that makes you a *Sapling* then." A little sneer curling at the edges of her mouth.

"I refuse to call myself that."

"Hear, hear." June looks around the room. "I hate these things. They're just adults trying to impress other adults. Nobody actually cares about anything. Like your dad. I bet he made you rehearse that stuff about sports. Am I right?"

"Every night for a month," I say. I take another long swig of my punch.

She shakes her head. "Typical. He probably doesn't know the first thing about you. You should tell him."

I look around to see the locations of the other Coles

(Dad and Mom won't leave Mr. Harrison's side and Nathan is being grilled by Richard and his cellist daughter, which I'm sure thrills my brother to no end). "That's easier said than done."

"Why's that?" June asks.

I lower my head.

"Alan." June leans over to my chair. "If you march straight over there and tell off your big, fat caveman of a father, I'll give you a kiss."

My stomach churns. "What? Wh-Why would—you don't have to—"

There's a brief moment where we look at each other, then June laughs, short and punchy. "Nah," she says. "You wouldn't want to kiss a bad girl like me anyway."

I need to put an air conditioner beneath my shirt. "Y-You don't seem like a bad girl."

"We've known each other for ten minutes. Anyway, everybody's bad in some way, aren't they? But everybody acts like they aren't, especially at big social functions like this. It's why I'm so bored tonight."

"Do you really think that? That everybody's bad in some way?"

"Of course," June says without hesitation. "Don't you?"

I squint. "Why would I think that?"

June rests a hand beneath her head and smiles. "Oh, I don't know. Your dad's clearly a disaster, for one thing. He looks like a serial killer—look at how he tries to smile. News flash: normal people do not smile like that. Your mom's totally broken, like she used to have a spine before your dad snapped it in two. Your brother clearly thought your dad's comment about artists was hilarious, so he's probably a delight to have at home."

My breath hitches. "Uh—"

"At school you're probably either ignored or bullied, based on how timid you are. If you have any friends, they've got to be rejects like you, with very poor social skills. Nobody gets you. Nobody except me." She raises a finger into the air. "People like us need to band together. We need to accept our badness and stand up together against everyone else. That's my mission statement: I am devoted to waking people up to the truth."

I gulp. Who in the world is this girl?

"I'm so glad I found you tonight," she says. "You can help me. Here's the plan." June reaches into her purse. "I've brought something very fun along tonight. But mischief is more fun when it's with a friend, don't you think?" She carefully pulls out a lumpy plastic bag.

"Uh . . . what's in there?" I ask, not sure if I want to know the answer.

She pushes her eyebrows together. "Hmm. Let's find out." She peels back a bit of the bag to reveal—

"Eepen!"

My voice squeals over the community center. Adults all around turn to look, but soon everyone goes back to their important grown-up business.

June raises an eyebrow. "Did you say 'eepen'?"

"J-June—that's—that is a—um—"

"I found it outside the building," she says. "It's great timing, since it's so hard to find dead rats these days. Well, apart from killing them yourself, I mean." She laughs, like she's told me a knock-knock joke, one that doesn't involve killing rats and/or carrying around their carcasses in her purse.

I glance around again, this time a little more desperately. "What are you going to do with that?"

"Well," June says, "I think the punch could use a little extra flavor, don't you?" She jerks her head in the direction of the food table. Her smile grows. "You can cover for me while I add our furry friend to the mix. Then everybody panics! All the dress-up and fake smiles go away in a heartbeat. We'll get to see how ugly everyone really is."

"I—I'm not doing that," I stammer. "That's—"

"Are you going to say that's *bad*?" June asks. "Well, of course it is. I already told you though: I'm a bad girl.

Everybody's bad, but I wear it on my sleeve. Now it's your turn. Prove your badness. Show your father he's not the boss of you."

Everything is happening too fast. I spin my head around the room—no adults near our table, nothing in between us and the buffet line, between us and that gigantic bowl of punch. "I'm not—" I start, then I say, "I thought you were cool."

June stops smiling. "You don't think I'm cool?"

"Not anymore I don't," I say.

She leans back in her chair, mouth slightly open.

"Don't do this," I continue. "What will your parents think? What's going to happen to—"

"Oh, this is cute," June says. The fun, playful side of her voice is paved over with a hardness, a coldness that I now realize was there all along. "You're trying to be *good*. Well, I've got a fun game for you: if you're really a good person, *stop me*."

We stare at each other for a few horrible moments. She smiles again. "Ta-ta," she says, then she sweeps onto her feet and power walks for the punch bowl.

My heart pounds, my blood pumps, my legs are ready to get up and run. But I'm frozen in place. There are so many people around, so many adults. She's almost at the punch bowl, the dead rat flopping at her side—she's really going to do it—

And I'm letting her.

Coward.

The next thing I know, my chair topples over behind me and I am running toward June and the punch bowl as the roadkill dangles dangerously above, and I flail my arms around without much of a plan, and I slip on a stray napkin and I smash into the table, and the punch bowl flies backward, and all of it splashes onto June, coating her from head to toe in purple drink.

My heart stops. My blood cools. My legs lock up. No one in the room is moving.

June shrieks. Dripping from head to toe, she wails, "Daaaaaaaaaddddddy!" at the top of her lungs. She levels a quavering finger at me.

A man comes running over to the table with a fistful of napkins as June cries out over and over, "Daddy, help! Daaaaaaaddddy!"

"June, June," says the man—oh my God, I know who this man is—"what happened?"

"W-We were talking and he told me he was really b-bored—and he brought this to stir up trouble"—she holds up the dead rat, every bit as soaked in punch as June, and everyone gasps—"and I tried to stop him, I really did, but I couldn't—and he—I'm soooooorrrryyy!"

Beneath June's damp hair, a dry eye stares at me.

I can't move. I can't breathe. I think I'm going to

faint. Everyone is watching, everyone is whispering, everyone is waiting to see what Mr. Harrison does about his daughter. Dad appears from nowhere to offer June tissues, and June bats at his hands and screams, "Get away from meeeee!" and runs out of the reception area, leaving a crushing silence in her wake.

"Mr. Harrison!" Dad says. "I—I'm so sorry! My son—he's not right in the head. When he gets stressed, he—"

"I think you and your family should go home, James," Mr. Harrison says quietly.

Dad arches his back. Promotion on the line or not, Dad is not a man who lets people talk to him like that. "If you think I'm going to—"

But maybe it's the fact that Mr. Harrison *is* his boss, or that he's surrounded by all his coworkers. Maybe he's just embarrassed. Whatever the reason, he ushers all four of us out of the Flower County Community Center without a fight, leaving all the world behind.

"I didn't—" I start, but Dad points to the car, and we pile inside, not a breath spent between us.

Dad doesn't start the car at first. He massages his temples a lot, and I keep bracing myself for him to open my door and tell me to get out and walk, or go die in a ditch, but eventually he starts the car. Mom grips the side of the car as we round turns. Nathan's eyes keep going back and forth between me and Dad, me and Dad.

When we get home, we file in for inspection, as we were before dinner. That's when Dad finally turns to me, finally drops the bombshell. "Your sketchbook," he says.

". . . what?"

"Your sketchbook," he says. "Now."

He turns around and, after some fiddling, lights the fireplace.

The flames flicker and dance in the mostly burned-out logs from last year. In them I can see reflected something dark, something disgusting. "Goldfish!" Dad barks. "Sketchbook."

"I . . . I . . . I—I—"

This isn't happening this isn't happening this isn't happening this isn't isn't isn't is NOT is NOT—

"Nathan," Dad says. "Your brother's sketchbook."

"Dad—" Nathan starts, but Dad turns back to the flames. The darkness he sees there, I begin to see.

Nathan looks at me. Looks at Dad. Me. Dad.

He slowly walks upstairs, and I let out a sob.

The wait is agony. The only noise is the crackling of the flames, and Dad rubbing his hands together. Then, slowly, descending footsteps from upstairs, and Nathan clutching my sketchbook, band tied around the sides. An entire year's worth of work and art, work and art that can never be replaced.

My cretpoj. My cretpoj that's going to change the world.

I've already started to cry. I try to muffle the noises, but there's no point. Big, heavy, stupid tears fall onto the carpet. I can't see anything through my tears, but when Nathan arrives, I try to look at Mom, who takes a step forward, until Dad glares at her, and she freezes in place. She clutches her cross to her neck and closes her eyes.

As Nathan hands the book to Dad, I cry, "Nathan!"

My brother looks me squarely in the eyes, then drops the book at Dad's feet.

Dad opens the gate to the fireplace nice and slow, clearly making sure I savor each second, remember each detail. Then he says, "You disappointed me."

And my sketchbook gets tossed in with the rest of the garbage.

I stay in front of the fireplace long after everyone else disappears, watching the little embers burn out, trying to remember as much as I can of my beautiful paintings.

Gone.

June was right after all.

I don't know what time it is before I trudge up the stairs to my empty room full of empty things. The stupid maple tree outside sways its stupid leaves. Who even cares? What's even the point?

Who even cares about my stupid cretpoj? My stupid project?

I almost climb into bed in my suit and coat—Mom draped the coat over my shoulders after who cares how long—because who even cares about stupid wrinkles, but I'm warm from being in front of the fireplace so long, so I at least take off the jacket and leave it, limp and lifeless, on my closet floor.

I sink into my closet and sit there. Just sit. I don't even think about anything. What is there to even think about? I figure, here's as good a place to sleep as any, so I slump onto my side, and I brush my head against something weird and lumpy and stupid. I go to move it out of the way and scrape my fingers against a bunch of pages of something.

Pages that feel used.

Slowly, slowly, slowly I look at the object.

This Sketchbook Belongs To:
Alan Cole

My hands tremble as I leaf through the pages. All my paintings—Big Green, raked leaves, apples and bananas—they're all here. And the last page, the outline of Connor's face, his big smile glowing up at me from the crinkled parchment, it's—it's—

I move the sketchbook to the side so my tears don't stain the paintings.

But—but I saw Nathan—

And it hits me.

He gave Dad my new sketchbook.

The empty one.

And Dad didn't know the difference.

My breath comes in loud gasps. I'm shaking. What in the world is going on?

I leave the sketchbook in my closet, where it'll have to hide for now. I look out my window at the maple—at Big Green—and the last thing I see before I fall asleep in my dress clothes is the swaying movement of the leaves, and the last thing I think before sleep bludgeons me over the head is maybe I've still got a lot to learn about people after all.

TWELVE

A dark, dreary cloud hangs over Sunday morning breakfast, like we're sitting at the kitchen table with the grim reaper hovering around, waiting to flash his scythe and cut us down. Nobody looks up when I walk in and quietly pour myself a bowl of Lucky Charms. I stare at Nathan, watching for some kind of reaction, some kind of sign about what he was thinking last night. Mom flips through the newspaper, but I can tell she sneaks some glances my way when I'm not looking. On my third spoonful, Dad says, "I'll have to grovel like a dog at Mr. Harrison's feet tomorrow."

I don't look up. Emphasis.

"What were you thinking?" he continues. "You embarrassed me."

When I woke up, I thought about what I'd say to Dad

when he inevitably started talking about this. I decided that, no matter what I said, he'd never believe me.

"Why are you such a bad kid?" Dad moans, massaging his temples. "Even Nathan wouldn't have done something like that."

So I go with my plan. "I'm sorry, Dad," I say quietly. Pattern.

"Sorry isn't good enough," he snaps. "I won't get my promotion. I might even lose my job. Then what'll I do?"

"I'm really sorry," I whimper, putting as much effort into it as I do when I'm trying to convince Nathan he's surprised me.

Dad raises his head. Upward movement. "You're done at that health club. Tell your friend to hang out with someone else."

At this, Nathan's eyes dart up. A fly on the canvas.

I knew Dad was going to say that. Still, I whine, "But Dad—"

My father growls, and it's enough to turn my spine to ice. "Think about what you did. It's all your fault. Everything. Understand?"

I nod. There it is again: in the blame game, I always come in first. Or maybe it's last. "Yes, Father."

Dad slowly gets up. "Get ready for church."

Mom pours me a glass of mango juice, my all-time favorite. Nathan, still a mystery, reads the paper. And I eat my Lucky Charms, ignoring the bubbling in my gut.

I'm going to the health club. I'm learning to swim.

Whether Dad knows about it or not.

Pattern breaking.

"Goodness," Madison says, his voice echoing around the Helen's Crest pool. "My parents could probably get these Harrison people a membership here, if that will help."

"Probably not," I say.

Sneaking out was a little tough. Even though Dad never pays attention to where me and Nathan are unless it's dinnertime, I still had to get my bike out of the garage after church, while Dad was working on some project. His power saw was so loud, I probably could've led a mariachi band through the garage and he wouldn't have noticed. (He still could've looked up and seen me, so I guess I got lucky.) And I'll even shower at the health club (fortunately they have private stalls) to hide the chlorine smell. This is how it's going to be, every day until CvC ends. I don't get to mark off "stand up to Dad" because Dad doesn't know about it, but CvC isn't why I'm doing it.

I'm doing it because he tried to destroy my cretpoj.

Madison says, "Well, you've had an adventure. It almost makes my weekend seem boring. Although I have to say, watching C-SPAN is never boring."

I snort. "Yeah. I bet."

Madison smiles, despite clearly trying not to. "I liked you better when you didn't talk. Now show me your flutter kick again."

Gripping my kickboard, I start splashing my legs, propelling myself toward the other side of the pool like a poorly constructed speedboat. I get about halfway there before I almost tip over, but I hold on to the kickboard, and I stay stable, and I make it to the other end.

"Good," Madison says, calling out as I swim back. "Now we'll try the backstroke. The swimming test is freestyle, backstroke, and breaststroke, but you won't be able to use the kickboard for any of them."

"Maddie!" a voice calls from the end of the pool.

Madison ducks down in the water. "We're a little busy."

Mrs. Dorothy Truman stands at the water's edge. "Come out of the pool, sweetie. I want to take a picture of you before you start losing weight."

Madison turns red. "That's, er, okay, Mom. I'm sure I'll remember what I looked like."

"Not for *you*," Mrs. Truman says. "For Aunt Grace and Great-Aunt Sylvia and your little cousins."

"Betty and Billy are *not* seeing this," Madison says. (His voice cracks on "not.")

"Oh, nutbutters," Mrs. Truman says. "I don't have my

phone on me. Is this your bag here on the bench, Anton? I'll go ahead and borrow yours."

I blink. "It's, uh, Alan. And that's okay—"

But Mrs. Truman already has my phone out, flipping fingers across the screen like she's squishing spiders. "Your phone is very disorganized, dear," she says. "When I'm done taking Maddie's picture I'll reorganize your apps."

Madison's head is bowed, and he's muttering under his breath what could be either prayers or swears.

"Stop pouting," Mrs. Truman says as Madison stands up to pose, looking completely miserable. "This will be another incentive to get you to lose all that weight. From the looks of it, Maddie, you need a few more incentives."

After texting the picture to her own phone, and doing Lord-knows-what to my music library, Mrs. Truman leaves, and Madison practically cannonballs back into the water. "Some help," he barks at me. "Taking pictures. And you let her!"

"What did you want me to do? She grabbed my phone herself." And I can't make the Trumans upset, because they might stop letting me come here.

He runs a wet hand over his hair. "You're lucky I'm a nice person. This only means I'll be tougher on you. Starting tomorrow, no kickboards."

My fingers instinctively squeeze the precious, protective foam. "Really?"

"You're pressed for time," he says. "The sooner you shed your training wheels, the better. But first: the backstroke. Let me show you the form."

As Madison positions me in the water, I stare up at the ceiling and wonder how Nathan's doing at swim practice, if he's got a Madison of his own to show him how to stay afloat.

"How are lessons coming?" Zack asks Monday at the Unstable Table.

We spent *hours* at Helen's Crest on Sunday. The muscles in my arms and legs feel like they've been flattened by a steamroller and left to dry out in the Sahara. "It's going well," Madison says after swallowing a bite of his salad. "Alan's a good student. Of course, he's got a good teacher too. Right?"

I nod. "Right."

You wouldn't be able to tell I'm a good student if you looked at me in the official swimming class at Evergreen, where Marcellus seems dedicated to undoing all the progress I've been making. I played dumb this morning and made sure to only follow Marcellus's "instructions," never to show him I'm actually learning something.

Of course, this is only part of it. I've still got to figure out how to make someone cry, which makes me squirm just thinking about. Or how to get my first kiss, which makes me squirm even worse. The vending machine is impossible. And even though I'm going behind Dad's back, it's a far cry from standing up to his face. But I can't think about all that, or about what happens if I don't beat Nathan. (If I do think about it, my brain threatens to melt.)

"That's great," Zack says. Then he immediately goes, "Hey, check this out." He takes the straw on his lunch tray and wedges it up his nostril. "Oday," he says, "Ib I do dis right I cad shood boogers oud."

"That's disgusting," Madison says. "We're trying to eat."

Zack yanks the straw out and wipes it on his shirt. "I was just showing something cool."

"Well, it's not cool," Madison says. "What does your father think when you come home and show him little stunts like that?"

"He doesn't think," Zack says. "He's dead."

All of Madison's muscles lock up.

"It's okay," Zack says. "If he was still around, I know he'd laugh too." He smiles.

Madison clears his throat. "I'm, er, sorry—"

Zack gasps. "That ceiling tile looks like a tumbleweed!"

Madison runs both hands over his hair. Repeatedly.

He looks at me. I shrug.

As we leave the Unstable Table after lunch, Zack calls my name. Madison lingers for a little bit, then he heads off to Miss Richter's room without us. Zack smiles when I come near. "Wanted to talk to about. That's No-Noun for, 'I wanted to talk to you about something.'"

"Madison didn't mean it," I say.

"Huh? Oh, I don't care about that. I need your help. See, I have this problem, and—wait, let's head over here, where it's quieter." He leads me out of the cafeteria—on the way I overhear a kid saying, "You could totally reach into that vending machine if you were tall enough"— and out a side door, clearly marked *DO NOT EXIT*, and suddenly we're outside, out of sight from the main hallway. He sighs and stretches his arms. "Muuuuch better."

I look around the small field in front of us. The amount of cigarette butts littering the grass says Zack isn't the only kid who knows about this secret exit. "I don't want to be late for class," I say.

Zack waves a hand. "This won't take long." Right, because Zack Kimble has such a strong concept of the passage of time. Before I can object even more, he takes a deep breath and says, "I've got a crush on someone."

"Oh," I say.

"Do you know Penny Schmidt?"

I shake my head.

Zack holds a hand to his heart. "She's perfect. She's nice and kind and sweet and good with animals and friendly to old people and she has glasses and her hair's in a bun and she has hazel eyes *like me* and when we get married we're going to buy famous paintings and keep them in our home and we won't even charge money to see them. That's Penny. I love her."

"Okay," I say slowly. "You probably shouldn't worry about getting married when you're twelve."

"It never hurts to plan ahead," Zack says. "Anyway, my problem is I can't talk to her. Every time I see her, I get so tongue-twisted I wind up saying something stupid. Can you imagine that? I really want to tell her how I feel, but the words get stuck inside me like a bowling ball inside a moose's throat. She might not even like me, but the odds are better than zero, right?"

"I guess," I say.

Zack shrugs. "If the odds are better than zero, that means there's hope. That means you shouldn't give up on it, no matter what. So the odds are better than zero she'll like me. Anyway, I thought we could help each other get confident enough to talk to our crushes."

My throat gets dry. "Uh, what?"

"Well, if I boost up your confidence it might help you talk to Connor, and if you boost mine it might make me talk to Penny, and then—"

"Shhhhhh!" I hold a finger to Zack's mouth and look around the empty field in a panic, like the cigarette butts have ears. "W-W-What are you talking about?" I whisper. "That's impossible."

"What?" Zack asks. "It's nothing weird."

The back of my shirt gets damp. How did—how is—this can't be—

"He doesn't know," Zack says. "I don't think anyone knows but me. It's obvious to me, because the way you get with Connor is like the way I'd get if Penny ever talked to me. I think it's great. Connor's a nice guy. You two would be happy together."

I'm breathing really heavy and my entire body feels weighted down with sandbags and—and—

"I won't tell anyone," Zack says, very gently. "But I think you should tell him how you feel. It's not fun living a secret life. That's why I try to be as open as possible with everyone."

Zack looks away from me, up at the clouds. He pulls something from his pocket: a small rock. He runs the stone along his fingers with an old, familiar rhythm. "My dad always told me be proud of who you are. He did a lot of kooky things. He liked to wear really silly hats. He went rock climbing all year round, even when it was snowing. Before he died he told me to never let anyone tell you you don't deserve to be who you are. The only person who can tell you that is yourself." He squeezes the rock. "I don't like it when people can't be themselves. That's why you should tell Connor."

My breathing calms down a little, but my voice still comes out raspy. "It's . . . not that easy."

"It usually isn't," Zack says. "But I'd rather have a hard time being myself than an easy time being somebody else."

Zack turns back around to me. He grins. "Wow, I feel better already! Thanks, Alan. You're a great friend. I know together we can really tell our special someones how we feel."

He heads for the door while I'm frozen in place. Then he stops and, in one awkward, fumbling motion, wraps me up in a hug. When I break free, he gives me a warm smile and heads back inside, leaving me standing in the cigarette-laden grass.

Why does everything have to be so complicated?

THIRTEEN

How would *you* get a gross, stained piece of paper out of a broken vending machine? I came up with three ideas:

1. Break the glass
2. Drill a hole in the back
3. Flip the machine upside down and hope the paper comes loose

Of course, Nathan says I can get the paper out without taking the machine apart or smashing anything. He promised. And I can't exactly turn the whole thing on its head since I am not, last time I checked, the Hulk. Or the Thing. Or the Hulking Thing Who Hulks Things. I'm me, and I can barely lift my algebra textbook.

Madison's come up with a few suggestions of his own:

4. Fix the machine and pay for the paper to come out
5. Ask Principal Dorset to open the machine for you
6. Get one of the Shrubs to flip the machine upside down and hope the paper comes loose

Problem is, I wouldn't even know where to start when it comes to fixing a vending machine, and with all my time outside of school pretty much taken up with fitness consultations, I don't have any way to learn. I guess I could follow Madison's train of thought and ask someone else for help, but I don't want to involve any more people than I already have. And there's no way Principal Dorset would help *me*, Mr. Where-Do-Babies-Come-From, and even if we could get somebody else to open it or even if someone else asked him instead of me, he'd still find out, and he'd put a stop to it before it could ever happen.

That leaves Zack's suggestions:

7. Take a paper towel roll, stick it into the bottom of the machine, and blow really hard
8. Play loud music on the floor; the bass will create vibrations that will dislodge the paper
9. Dump pool balls onto the bottom, then do shots with a cue stick until one of the balls goes flying onto the paper, dislodging it

10. Let a mouse loose in the machine and wait for him to return with the paper

11. Make "paper magnets" by taping bits of paper to the ends of magnets

12. Key in the secret code that automatically opens up all the rings, even when the machine is turned off

I shouldn't have to tell you why none of those would work.

And there's also this bonus problem of not only finding a solution that works, but finding one I can pull off while there's a zillion people around. The vending machine is in the middle of a main hall, after all, and I can't exactly go messing around with wiring or dumping mice in the bin in the middle of a school day. After school doesn't work either—like I said, all my free time is basically going to be spent in the pool, trying kickboard-free strokes. But is that me making an excuse for not being smart enough?

Here I am, Alan Cole, the boy who got beat by a vending machine.

"Coming, Alan?" Miss Richter calls from her room. Sighing, I stop staring at the machine and walk into Miss Richter's room. The three-sided square of desks is empty now, and Miss Richter lords over papers as she sips her coffee thermos. "Don't be late for detention, please," she says.

Detention. The word conjures up scary images of being locked in a jail cell, forced to write *I shall be a good, obedient child* four hundred times or until your wrist falls off, whichever comes first. They say your first one's the hardest. After that, it gets easier, and before you know it, you have a criminal rap sheet the size of *Discovering America*, and you're setting off stink bombs in the teachers' lounge.

"Where's Talia?" I ask, taking my usual seat.

"She took her detention this morning with Mrs. Ront," Miss Richter says. "It's just you and me."

"What do we do in detention?"

"*We* don't do anything," she says, finally looking at me. "*You* sit quietly and do your homework, and *I* sit quietly and grade things. It's an exhilarating time, really."

I nod. I open up my science homework, ready to memorize more elements on the periodic table, but before I get very far, Miss Richter says, "Or I could give you a special project."

A special project? "What is it?"

"I could use some help cleaning and sorting things. If you want to work on your homework though, that's fine."

Doing mindless work like this might free up my brain

to think about the vending machine more. "I'll help you," I say.

I kind of hope I get to use Miss Richter's extendable pointer, but instead she sets me up with some whiteboard cleaner and a rag. When I squeeze the spray nozzle, I gag a little. "This smells horrible."

"I never said the job was glamorous," Miss Richter says. "Make sure to mention all the abuse I've put you through at your parent-teacher conference tomorrow."

The bottle of cleaner makes a dull thud as I drop it on the floor. "Parent-teacher conference? T-Tomorrow?"

Miss Richter raises both eyebrows. "They're scheduled to run all week for ASPEN Saplings. You're supposed to come in with a parent tomorrow night. Tell me you didn't forget."

Well, *forget* is the wrong word. More like, bury it in my brain and hope it went away forever.

"You've been acting a little distracted for a few days now, Alan. Is everything okay?"

I swallow. "Yeah, everything's fine."

She watches me for a few more seconds, then goes back to her papers. Slowly I pick up the cleaner and rag and start wiping again. Dad will want to come. He always wants to put on a good impression. But maybe I can snag Mom instead. Maybe Dad will be so mad at me he won't want anything to do with me. I did manage to keep my detention, my induction into the Evergreen Troublemakers Hall of Fame, quiet from him. The last thing I need is for Dad to have any more reasons to be disappointed in me.

The fireplace dances in my eyes, the flames searing, ripping, destroying. I shudder and get back to wiping.

After a little while of me spraying and cleaning, Miss Richter asks from her desk, "Who's your hero, Alan?"

I stop. "My hero?"

"Yeah," she says. "I want to do a unit on heroes across history. Who do you aspire to be like? Who inspires you?"

"Uh," I say. "I don't know."

"There's nobody? Nobody you look at and think, this is who I want to become like?"

Is there? I mean, I really admire some artists, like Picasso, but I've never thought of them as heroes. I don't really look up to anyone I know personally. But is it really okay for a twelve-year-old boy to not have a hero? Isn't it some kind of sacrilege, a sin against the commandments of being a kid?

"Maybe Batman?"

Right when it comes out I turn red. Come on—a comic book character? Miss Richter doesn't laugh though. Instead she asks, "Why is Batman your hero?"

"I guess he's really tough, and he's got lots of cool stuff, and—I don't know, Miss Richter, I've never really thought about this before."

"Hmmm," Miss Richter hums, drumming her fingers on her desk. "Could you ever see yourself fighting crime alongside Batman? He has sidekicks, doesn't he?"

Alan the Robin. I used to fantasize about that, about flying away into the sky and starting a life of spectacular crime-fighting and bright, flashy costumes and gadgets and—

"No," I say. "I could never do that. I'm not a hero." I scrub at a patch of grime on the whiteboard.

Miss Richter stops talking for a bit. Then she asks, "Do you know what an introvert is, Alan?"

"An animal without a spine," I say glumly.

"That's an invertebrate. An introvert is somebody who gets drained by being around people and energized by being by themselves. If you're the opposite, you're an extrovert. Which one do you think you are?"

"Definitely the first one."

"I'd say so," my teacher continues. She takes a sip of her coffee. "People often think the only way to be a hero is to be an extrovert, because they work better around people. But introverts can problem solve too. Just because you're not going out fighting crime in long underwear doesn't mean you can't be a hero. You don't need superpowers to be super. Or a good kid. Remember that, Alan."

I polish the last bit of grime on the board. "Batman doesn't have superpowers."

"Exactly." Miss Richter sounds like her whole argument was leading up to that point, but I'd be willing to bet my teacher doesn't even know the difference between the Joker and the Riddler. Still . . .

She walks over to the board as I set the chemical-smelling cleaner on the floor. "Looks like it was bought yesterday," she says.

I raise my head and she's looking at me, smiling. She's young for a teacher, but she's already got lines by her mouth and eyes, and she barely wears any makeup, and her hair's kept short, and her eyes . . . her eyes give off this *light*. I'd probably do that with shading around the bottom of her eyelids to emphasize the brightness inside her eyes, and maybe some focus on the upper half of her face, and I realize right then and there I don't know Miss Richter's first name, I don't know the first thing about her apart from the fact that she's my homeroom and social studies teacher, but if I look at her face long enough I'll—I'll—

"Alan?" she says. "Earth to Alan?"

"You're right," I say. "You don't have to be loud to change the world. You just need to—"

I trail off once I realize I don't actually know *what* you need to do. But my half answer seems good enough for Miss Richter, who smiles again and says, "See what happens when you listen to your teachers? You actually learn things. Who knew? Now come on, help me sort these papers. . . ."

FOURTEEN

By the time I get home from Helen's Crest, after my detention, it's almost dinnertime. I run into Marcellus on the way out the door—Nathan never likes to expose his friend to our family's unique eating environment. Marcellus stops in front of the door, looks me over, and nods. Then he's on his way. I wonder what goes on in his mind sometimes, what he does when he isn't taking orders from Nathan.

I need to ask Mom about the parent-teacher conference, but I ran late with Madison and I didn't have time to shower at the club, so if I don't hop in the shower right now, Dad will smell the chlorine, and I'll be up dirt creek without any stain remover. So I take the world's fastest shower, but it's still not fast enough—Dad's already at the table when I get out, and Mom's serving up dinner.

Dad's eyes study me for a bit as I sit down, but he digs right into his food.

Okay, not a problem. I can ask Mom after dinner, when Dad's not around, so he won't know about it. Problem solved.

"Hey, Al," Nathan says at the table, spitting bits of food over his plate, "who's going to your parent-teacher conference tomorrow?"

It's like someone hurls a kickball into my gut at ninety miles an hour. I'm grateful I'm not swallowing anything right now, because otherwise our tablecloth would be decorated with half-digested fried chicken.

"Parent-teacher conference?" Dad asks.

"Oh, uh," I stammer. Think fast, think fast, think fast. "Mom's going."

Mom blinks a few times, then looks up.

"You're going?" Dad asks Mom. "You've got a church fund-raiser tomorrow."

She looks at me. Whatever my face looks like, it makes her blink a few more times. "I can't," she mumbles, tearing herself back to her plate. "I've got the fund-raiser."

Dad chuckles. Not the normal kind of chuckling you do when you're actually happy, because Dad's never happy. The kind you do when you're a hawk, and you're about to bite into a nice, juicy piece of prey. "What time is this conference?"

Lie to him lie to him come up with some excuse don't don't don't don't—

"Six at night," I say.

"I expect a good report from your teacher," Dad says. "Don't disappoint me again."

The flames dance behind Dad, licking everything nearby.

It's not easy painting when you've got a lot on your mind.

It's not easy painting when you're busy worrying about what Dad's going to hear tomorrow, and what Dad's going to *do* tomorrow.

It's not easy painting when you're wondering about introverts, and if you could really be a hero when you can't even stand up for yourself.

It's not easy painting when you don't know what your brother is doing, whose side he's on, what he's plotting next.

You guess you could ask him yourself. It'd be easy, since he just walked into your room. "Nice sketchbook," he says.

You—I mean, I—stash it under my desk, but he shakes his head. "I'm not the one you should hide that from," he says.

"Why?" I ask. "Why did you—"

"Don't get the wrong idea, Al," Nathan says. "We're

not bosom buddies or anything like that. I chose you over Dad, that's all. Tonight was a little reminder we're still opponents. What happened with that girl at the dinner anyway?"

I give Nathan a curious look. Is he actually . . . reaching out? "She was fine when she started talking—"

"Oh wait," Nathan says. "I don't care anymore. Whatever she did to you, you deserved it. You made Dad worse, so you probably made her worse too. How's the ol' CvC coming? Done anything new?"

I sigh. Guess not. "I'm working on stuff," I say.

Nathan hops onto my bed and bounces up and down; the springs creak with the impact of his feet. He takes my blanket and ties it around his neck like a cape. "I had my first swim team practice today. I'll ace that test in no time. And that'll be all I'll need to do, since you won't get anything else done. I was thinking: who's this friend of yours Dad mentioned?"

Oh crap. "He's nobody," I say fast, too fast. "Just a kid I know from class."

"You must be on pretty good terms with him if he's letting you share some fancy health club," Nathan says. "What are you really doing there, I wonder? You don't care about exercise. Is this friend named . . . Vic?" He waggles his eyebrows.

This isn't where I expected this to go. Evergreen is so

big, and Nathan goes so far out of his way to avoid being seen with me unless he needs something, that he's never seen me with Madison or Zack. If he thinks I'm going to the club with "Vic Valentino," then he won't know Madison actually exists, unless he sees me with Madison and assumes Madison is Vic, but if he *doesn't* think I'm going there with Vic I'll have to tell him why I'm going—think fast, Alan—

"None of your business," I say to buy some time.

The hyena laughs. "I knew it. You're working out with your little boyfriend. That's cute. I wonder what he'd think if he knew how you really felt? How you pine for him. How you *yearn* for him. How you can't live without him. You're madly in love. We should call this CvV, since you'll change your last name to Valentino soon enough, right?"

I gulp. "Y-Yeah. I'm going with Vic. We've been biking there every day."

"Ha!" Nathan laughs. He hops off my bed and tosses the blanket from his neck and lets it fall clumsily over my head. "You can't hide anything from me, Boy Blunder. If you don't want to scare Vickie away, better up your game. We're so close to the finish line—let's not ruin the ending, right?"

"Right," I say, trying to keep the relief from my voice.

As he leaves my room, Nathan looks back and—and

doesn't smirk. "Good luck tomorrow," he says in a low voice.

I take a nice, long breath. Whatever's up with Nathan, he still doesn't think I'm clever enough to lie to his face. I just hope he doesn't see me talking to Madison or Zack and make some nasty assumptions about them.

Or hurt them.

I almost grab my sketchbook from under my desk and get back to painting Connor's hair, but there's a knock at my door.

Nobody knocks at my door.

"Come in?" I say.

And in walks Mom, holding a plastic bag. Her eyes move about my room like she's exploring a dusty tomb, untouched by man for centuries. She shuts the door behind her.

"I'm sorry," Mom says.

"It's okay," I reply. "You've got something at church tomorrow anyway."

"No," she says. "Your book."

Oh.

Mom hands me the plastic bag. Slowly, fingers quavering, I reach inside to find a new sketchbook. It's not quite the same as the one she bought me before the school year started, but it's still a brand-new sketchbook, full of potential.

"He shouldn't have done that. And I shouldn't have . . ." She clucks her tongue and turns to leave. "Be careful with it."

"Wait," I say, but I don't know what I want to ask. There's so much to say, so much that's gone unsaid.

She stops, hand on my doorknob, and sighs. "Your grandparents never wanted this."

"What?" I ask, rolling my chair forward.

Mom sighs. "Family's supposed to be everything. But your grandparents didn't treat your father right."

I lean in. I've never heard anything about my grandparents before. Heck, I've never even heard anything about Mom and Dad's life before they had Nathan and me.

"We shouldn't talk about them like this," Mom continues. "But your father felt unloved. They were teachers, and he wasn't a strong student. His best was never enough, no matter how hard he tried. They pushed and pushed him, and eventually they pushed him away. As soon as he could, he left them behind to make a name for himself. *We* left. We were happy. Until your grandparents—they—"

My mother raises her head to the ceiling, still facing away from me. "They died. You had just started kindergarten. Their old family motto was 'Today, do your best,' but no one wished him that growing up, and they certainly weren't going to wish him that now. He turned his back on that motto. He swore to always put himself first, no matter what."

Whenever Dad's told me to do my best, it was always to make *him* look good. My voice comes out very thin. "Why don't you ever talk about this?"

"Dad has so much pain in his heart," Mom says. "He thought everyone in his family was so much smarter than him. He knew he could never compete with his parents, or with you or Nathan, even though you're only kids."

She finally turns to face me. She looks me up and down, then shuts her eyes. No tears. "You look just like him."

I swear, even from up here, I can hear the ticking of the wooden clock. I clutch the new sketchbook to my chest.

"That's his story," Mom says.

"What about you?" I ask. I want to find out everything I can before she retreats into her shell. "What's your story, Mom?"

She smiles. A sad, humorless smile. "This is my story," she says, gesturing around her. "You and Nathan are my story. Your father is my story." She falls silent.

Not every story has a happy ending.

"But what about your parents?" I ask, remembering

the special cross Mom wore to the dinner. "Why don't you ever talk about them?"

"Your dad wants me to focus on happier times," she says softly.

I have to pick my jaw up off the floor. How can Dad force her to break off contact with her own family? Then I remember the phone call Mom was having the other night, when I thought she was talking to Denise, when she got paranoid after she thought I was listening in. I wonder what else my mother is hiding.

"Maybe now you understand him more," Mom continues.

"I understand him more, yeah," I say, unable to stop myself. "But I don't think that's an excuse."

"You should show Dad respect—"

"He burned it."

Mom wrings her hands together.

"Mom," I say. "Don't—" I swallow.

Her hands are squeezed together so firmly they turn shock-white. "Before Dad left home, your grandmother tried to make amends. She told him, 'Today, do your best.' It was too late though, and he left without saying good-bye. They always invited him up to their lakeside cabin every summer. But one year there was an awful accident, and they drowned."

". . . what?"

I don't have time to teach you.

We're never going to the ocean anyway, so why even bother?

No more swimming. It's bad enough you're doing it in school, but now you're doing it for fun too? No more swimming!

"I—" I open my mouth. "I never—he never—"

"I never told you," Mom whispers. "That was when everything changed. We were supposed to finally go up to the lake to visit, but you had gotten sick after you kept the window open all night painting that picture of a sunset. Dad got sick too. He thought maybe if he'd been there, he could've . . ." She closes her eyes. "I think he still blames you."

My earliest memory comes rushing back. Me sick in bed, Dad screaming at me, "This is all your fault"—is that really it? Is that when everything fell apart?

Mom inches the door open. "Be careful, Alan." And she's gone.

He could have had different reasons for not wanting to teach us. Maybe it brought up too many bad memories. Maybe he didn't want to go near the water himself, that's how traumatized he was. Maybe he didn't want to teach us a valuable life skill out of spite.

Maybe he was trying to protect us.

Maybe sometimes people act like they're doing things

for selfish reasons, like not teaching their kids how to swim, or maybe they try to downplay the good things they do, like protecting a sketchbook, but they're really looking out for you.

Maybe sometimes people retreat from their families because they're scared of the world, so they hold their love in a tight ball and bury it deep inside. Maybe there's hope for even those people too.

Maybe.

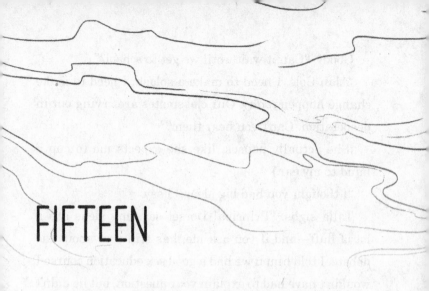

FIFTEEN

I'm the first one to board bus 19 on Tuesday, as usual. This is Nathan's second day of swim practice, so he's been biking to school instead of carpooling with Marcellus. I look out the window as we mosey on over to Evergreen and I watch the cars zoom past. Are the people inside introverts or extroverts? Do they have fiery darkness inside them? Are they being true to themselves? What would a cretpoj of them look like? Am I—

"Alan Cole," a voice says next to me. "Scooch."

Talia doesn't wait for me to actually move, shimmying onto the seat and practically forcing me over to the side. "Good morning," I grumble.

My class president nods stiffly. "This isn't a social call. As the leader of our class, I'm conscripting you for an assignment."

Goody. "Can it wait until we get to school?"

"Alan Cole, I need to make a splash. I need to make change happen *today*. Our classmates are crying out in desperation. Can't you hear them?"

(She actually pauses, like she expects me to cup a hand to my ear.)

"I thought you had big ideas," I say.

Talia sighs. "Principal Dorset says my ideas are a lot of fluff—and if you ask me, he's still sore about the debate. I told him if we had a good sex education course I wouldn't have had to explain your question, but he didn't want to hear it. So I need something big."

"I don't know," I say. "Why are you asking me?"

Here she hesitates. "You're the only one who listens when I talk."

Oh.

"Except when you don't," she says, the steel returning to her voice. "You forgot about the favor, didn't you?"

"The what?"

She shakes her head. "Unbelievable. Alan Cole, you are unbelievable. The favor I owe you over the election. You'd better come up with something soon, or the offer goes away. I'm a busy girl and I don't have time to wait around for indecisive boys."

I completely forgot about that. With everything that's happened since Friday, Talia and her weird favor haven't even been on my mind at all. "Well, do you know how to break into a vending machine?"

Talia gasps. "Alan Cole! I'm Sapling class president! Unbelievable! If I ever hear about you trying to damage a vending machine, I'll tell Principal Dorset. Don't test me. Unbelievable!"

"It's not like that," I protest. "It's hypothetical."

"Well, take your hypothetical scenarios and march them off this bus right now. You know, I don't even think we should have vending machines in school. They encourage obesity. I've already talked with Principal Dorset about getting rid of that broken one outside Miss Richter's room—"

"No!" I choke out. "That one's, uh, got to stay. For sentimental reasons. Yeah."

Talia sighs. "Alan Cole, you're a strange boy. That machine's days are numbered. Did you know someone shoved a dirty piece of paper inside? We can't have things like that clogging up the halls. I'm glad you agree with me."

Great. That's the last thing I need—Talia tossing out the vending machine, paper and all. She can do whatever she wants after Friday, after I solve Nathan's riddle. Somehow.

When I get off the bus, kids start giving me funny looks. At first I think it's still leftovers from my question at the debate, but these are different looks, like they're trying to figure something out, like I'm a missing piece of a weird jigsaw puzzle.

"What's going on?" Madison asks at my locker. "I heard a rumor about the pool, but nothing specific."

"Maybe they canceled swimming forever," I say, letting the pleasant thought float through my head.

Madison taps his chin. "Hmmm. Unlikely. It sounds like something happened to a student this morning."

"Alan!" Zack yells from the other end of the hall, sprinting past Mrs. Ront ("No running!") and a group of older kids ("Watch it, Nesthead!") before stopping in front of us. "Did you hear?" he pants, grabbing his side. "It's—"

Then he freezes completely, like a deer on a highway, as a girl walks over. Her face is bunched up in a bushy scarf, despite the fact it's only October. She keeps her head ducked but clearly makes a beeline for us. Zack literally jumps behind me and pokes his head out from my side.

"Um," the girl says quietly. "Hello, Alan."

I sort of recognize her. I think she's in my art class, but I don't know her name. "Hi," I say.

"Hello," Madison says. "I'm Madison Wilson Truman, Alan's friend and life coach. Who might you be?"

Behind me, Zack gulps. "Hi, Penny."

Penny Schmidt only has eyes—hazel eyes—for me. She ignores Zack and Madison and says to me, "I heard about your brother. That's, um, pretty scary, huh?"

"What?" I ask. "What do you mean?"

"That's what I came to tell you!" Zack says, stepping out from behind me. "I heard some guys talking about it in the bathroom—your brother almost drowned!"

My heart pounds in my chest like a timpani. "*What?*"

"I heard he's fine," Penny says. "But I bet he's pretty embarrassed."

Madison crosses his arms. "Why would he be embarrassed? There's nothing wrong with not knowing how to swim."

Penny whispers, "There's something wrong with diving into the deep end and not knowing how to float and needing Coach Streit to give you mouth-to-mouth."

Madison's eyes bug out. "Why on earth would he dive into the deep end if he's still learning?"

"Because he thinks he can do anything," I say, breathing a little easier. "So he's okay then?"

"He definitely won't want to show his face for a while," Penny says quietly. "Now everyone knows him as the boy who almost drowned and made out with Coach Streit."

Zack laughs, really forced. "Ha! Good one, Penny. You're so funny."

Penny smiles but doesn't look at Zack. Instead she

looks at me. "I guess we know who the cool one in the family is."

When she walks away after I don't say anything to her weird comment, I'm left holding on to my algebra textbook, weighing me down even more than usual. He almost died . . . but he's okay.

"Oh no," Madison says quietly. "Do you know what this means, Alan? He's winning. He's ahead of you in points."

"He's—huh?"

"He's the most well-known kid in school now, isn't he?" Madison asks. "Everyone's talking about him."

Zack gasps. "And he kissed Coach Streit. He got his first kiss! That counts, right?"

"CPR is *not* a first kiss," I grumble. The idea's so absurd I can't imagine anyone arguing it seriously.

Except Nathan. He'll try and spin this around like he had it all planned, like even though he won't learn to swim he traded one CvC task for two. Nathan Cole, genius mastermind. And because CPR is called the kiss of life, he'll argue it counts. This is what he used to do in other CvC games: find loopholes. I'm always powerless to stop it. Which means, indeed, he's up four to two.

Once we walk into homeroom, Connor nods at me as he looks over science notes. "Hey, man. I hope I do okay on this quiz today. This chemistry stuff is tough."

I plonk down in my seat, doing my best not to think about how much harder I'm going to have to practice at Helen's Crest—if that's even possible—or how mean I'd have to actually be to make someone cry. "Hey."

"Man, Ron's got it easy," Connor says. "He's in the slow classes. All they care about is if you show up."

I almost say, *it'd be nice if Ron stopped showing up*, but I don't. Instead I shrug.

"You okay?" Connor asks. "Hey, if you're still upset about Ron saying that stuff to you, don't take it personally. He's a good guy. Even if he's gay."

"Uh . . . w-what?"

Connor laughs. "Yeah. He's a little punk. He's probably got some gay little crush on me and that's why he acts like such a tough guy. What do you call that—overcompensating?"

"Yeah . . . overcompensating."

"You know what I mean? The homo's hopeless. He's so gay. Right?"

Something inside me, in a place closer to the surface than I thought, gets a chip in it. "R-R-Right," I whisper.

Connor's smile gets big. "See? I knew you'd get it." He pops his gum and goes back to his notes, looking over a formula scrawled in messy handwriting.

I sit in my desk, trying hard not to let those words fire around my brain like a machine gun, popping holes in the gray matter. Trying hard and failing. So what if he says "gay" like that? So what if he thinks Ron has a "gay little crush" on him? Lots of guys trash talk like that. It doesn't mean he wouldn't be interested in—in—

In my pocket, my phone vibrates. With a trembling hand I read the text message:

u shold tlel him

To my left, Zack gives me a goofy smile.

I quickly tap out a reply:

you should get a reality check.

Zack frowns. He starts typing something else, but the bell rings, and the phones get put away, and I realize maybe Zack's not the only one who needs a reality check.

After homeroom I'm summoned to Principal Dorset's office. He explains how Nathan was rushed to the emergency room this morning, how our family has been notified (meaning Mom, thank God, so here's hoping she does what she does best and keeps quiet), and how Nathan will be home the rest of the day. So he's fine, and that's what matters.

I kind of doubt he'd say the same about me, but hey.

I have art right before lunch, and today Mrs. Colton gives us a lecture on perspective, which is basically how you make distance and dimensions in a two-dimensional drawing. We try sketching out an image of a street stretching into the horizon. Across the art table, I notice Penny Schmidt for the first time. I wonder: What does Zack see in her? What does somebody like Zack look for in a crush? Maybe I should be taking notes. (Then again, I don't know if *Zack* should really be doling out romance tips.)

Mrs. Colton hums a little song as she flits about the room, offering feedback and suggestions to everyone. "Nice shading, Omar. You could tighten up the lines there and really make it eye-popping, Shannon. Rudy, I don't think streets have googly eyes, but I've never said no to creativity before. Alan—"

She stops at my seat and looks down at my paper.

Blank.

My teacher sighs. "Alan," she says quietly, "all you need to do is draw a street. You have free rein. Isn't that liberating?"

"I'm sorry," I whisper.

When Mrs. Colton walks away I reach into my backpack and pull out my old sketchbook, and I turn to the last page, where Connor's half-painted big smile beams up at me. There's a deep tightness in my chest as I stare back at my crush. Then, like tugging off a Band-Aid, I rip the page out of my sketchbook and crumple it up into a little ball. Unlike tugging off a Band-Aid, it isn't any easier to do it fast. The tightness doesn't go away. In fact, it expands, and it threatens to pop out of my eyes and throat, and it's all I can do to keep it bottled inside.

Oh wait, I'm in class. Whoops.

I look around to make sure nobody's watching, but everyone's busy putting gravel on their streets or something. Except Penny, who looks back down at her paper when I catch her eye.

After a big, fat zero from Mrs. Colton, class wraps up, and there's a storm cloud over my head, raining lightning bolts onto my earlobes. I can hardly get out of the art room, normally my favorite spot in all of Evergreen, fast enough. Before I get far though, somebody taps me on the shoulder.

"Um, hi," Penny says when I turn around.

Oh God, she's going to ask me what's wrong, why did I crumple my paper, is everything okay, why are you so upset about your *gay little crush* . . . "Hi."

Penny shifts her feet as the noisy crowd flows by. I should really tell her about Zack. Maybe it'll help him break the ice if she knows how he feels. "Uh," I say, "my friend—"

Before I know it, she stumbles forward with her eyes closed and her lips out and her bushy scarf scrapes my chin and *oh my God we are on full alert here, battle stations at the ready, Code Red repeat we have a Code Red this is not a drill THIS IS NOT A DRILL—*

I scream about three octaves higher than usual and dash halfway down the hall by the time I come to my senses. Laughter comes from *everywhere*.

That was—she was—she wanted to—she—and me—

Something tells me that's not how that's supposed to go.

Someone who isn't me might have said, *Oh hey, I'd love to swap spit with you in broad daylight when anyone can walk by, especially since I basically met you today and my friend has a crush on you. Oh, and also, I've got it bad for a homophobe. That's cool, right?*

I wasn't thinking of any of that at the time though. At the time, I just panicked.

Come on, you would've panicked too.

Humor me a little, all right?

When I get to the cafeteria, I walk on tiptoes, because there's this nagging dread that bubbles up that somehow, some way, I've done something bad. And maybe I have—Penny probably feels really stupid. But you better believe I'm not about to go up to her and do a group hug and toast some marshmallows.

Could've checked off another task, a Nathan-esque voice in my head says. *Nobody'll ever want to kiss you ever again. Too bad, huh, Al?*

A spit-filled blatty fart noise fills my ears. I spin around and say, "Knock it off, will you?"

Zack leans back. "Oh. Sorry."

I take a deep breath. "I'm sorry. You . . . scared me, that's all."

He shrugs. "It's okay. I thought of another idea for the vending machine. We take the machine to a river and send it downstream. When it fills with water, the paper will fall out. Nobody said it had to be in one piece, right? It'll clean off the paper too!" He gives a thumbs-up, then goes on about this until we finally get seated, finishing with, "Salmon swim upstream, so we might have to worry about them—"

As I put fried chicken from last night's dinner in with the cafeteria's mac and cheese, I feel someone standing at the edge of the table. I look up and immediately turn bright red.

"Penny," Zack squeaks. "What a surprise! Hey, you can have a seat, there's a seat right next to me—"

"You're not as cool as I thought," Penny says.

I huddle into my shoulders. "What do you mean?" Zack asks.

She ignores him. "I thought you were really funny after the debate. And I like your hair. But you humiliated me." She scowls. "You didn't have to scream so loud, like I was some ugly freak. All I wanted was a kiss."

That Nathan-esque voice pipes up again, *She's only a few steps away from crying. Seal the deal, Al!* I squeeze my eyes closed and tap my temples until the voice shuts up.

"Now, hang on," Madison says. "If you want my honest opinion, I hardly think the cafeteria is the place for this sort of juvenile romantic talk—"

"Cram it, tubby," Penny spits.

Madison turns pale and puffs out his cheeks, but he doesn't say anything. Zack pipes up, "Penny! I don't know what happened, but let me help—"

"Admit it," Penny says to me. "You're a loser like your brother. A big loser."

I don't know what it is. Maybe it's the comparison to Nathan. Maybe it's *tubby*. Maybe it's how she practically assaulted me and then blamed *me* for not doing anything back. Maybe it's all three. Whatever it is, it fires me up. My heart rages. My blood boils. My temper flares. I look Penny Schmidt square in the eyes and open my mouth to say the coolest, cleverest comeback I can muster.

"Takes one to know one."

Plop.

That's the sound of my coolness level hitting rock bottom and splattering all over the place like a wet dog turd.

Penny giggles. "Wow, cool guy. I guess you really showed me. I'll see you around, loser."

Zack stands up. "Penny, wait! You don't have to be

mean! I know you're good on the inside. You must be having a bad day—I—I wanted to tell you something—"

"Probably not the best time," I whisper.

But Zack keeps going on. "I—I've always—thought you and me could—well, that we—"

Now Penny laughs a full-blown, snorty laugh, one that echoes across the cafeteria. Around us, everyone quiets. "You're kidding, right? You? I can't be seen with you. Everyone'll think I'm even more of a—" She pauses, then says, "You're the biggest loser in school. You're such a loser you make other losers seem cool. The only way you'd ever find a girl willing to go out with you would be if she were blind and deaf, so she'd never actually be able to see for herself how much of a loser you are. Nobody wants to be around you, and no one ever will. You should crawl into a hole and die, then at least we wouldn't have to look at you."

Zack sits back down.

Penny looks around, as if only now realizing how loud she was. She huddles into her scarf and shuffles off to the other end of the cafeteria. She looks back three times, but I can't tell who she's looking at.

"Er," Madison says. "Zack?"

Zack stares down at his lunch tray, unmoving.

"You're not a loser," I say. "She's wrong."

"Yes, of course," Madison says. "You're really very cool. Everyone knows it."

He doesn't move. Doesn't even blink.

I take a deep breath, get really close to his ear, and make a weird squawking noise. "Teach that to your turtle."

A little smile appears on Zack's face. He blinks a few times.

I give him a thumbs-up. I don't need to say anything else.

"I guess it wouldn't have really worked out, huh?" he says.

"That girl was horrible," Madison says. "You can do better."

"But I told her, and that's what matters," Zack says, looking right at me. "And she's right: I am a loser."

"Don't say that," Madison says, shaking his head. "You're not—"

"I am," Zack says; his voice wavers a little. "And you know something? It doesn't matter. Who cares if you're cool or not? Who cares if you win or lose? I know who I am. And I'm a big, fat loser!" Zack yells this last bit, spinning around his chair. People look over, and a teacher mutters something to another teacher, but I know Zack doesn't care. He's still spinning, hands raised, yelling,

"Wheeeee!" as he turns around and around. When he finally stops, he wipes his eyes and asks, "But . . . you guys still want to be my friends, even though I'm a loser, right?"

I nod. "Losers have to stick together."

Zack looks at Madison, who fidgets. "Er," he stammers. "I only have space on my calendar for one friend."

"Madison, come on," I say.

He sighs. "Fine."

Zack reaches across the table and grabs Madison's shoulder. "That's an across-the-table hug," Zack says. "When lunch ends, I'll give you a real one."

"I can hardly wait," Madison says, but I see the small smile he tries to hide.

Zack puts his hand in the center of the table, thumb raised. I do the same, touching fists, and Madison is the last in. "Losers, now and forever," Zack says.

"Losers together," I say.

"Losers and their slightly less-of-a-loser friend," Madison says.

As we leave the cafeteria, I watch Zack. His bouncy step, his straight back, the way his hand clutches something rock-shaped in his pocket. His eyes are wide, and full, and hopeful. He comes over and whispers to me, "I'm wearing him."

"Huh?"

"Officer Orville. I wore him for the first time today. That's why I wanted to tell Penny."

"I guess luck wasn't on your side then."

Zack gives me a big grin. "No. It was."

SIXTEEN

SIXTEEN

At Helen's Crest, I can barely support myself against the wall, that's how tired my arms are. But Madison isn't having any excuses. "Let's run through the test. One length freestyle, half-length backstroke, half-length breaststroke."

"I think I'm going to pass out."

"Hmph." Madison shakes his head, bobbing with the rhythm of the water. "That's because you're not breathing properly. I keep telling you, don't hold your breath so often. Inhale with your mouth when your head's above water, and exhale with your nose when it's under. If you get lost, think about breathing regularly. Inhale, exhale. In, out. Go on, practice the test."

I know better than to argue with my coach. Steeling

myself, I kick off from the wall and launch into a free-style kick.

When I first started coming here, I could barely support myself on a kickboard. Now, over a few days of really intense practice, I can make it to the other end of the pool. But can I come back with the breaststroke? Madison keeps saying the breaststroke is easy, but I can't get the form down, and even though you're supposed to keep your head above water most of the time in the breaststroke, I keep looking down and inhaling a world of chlorine.

I make it to the far end of the pool, then flop onto my back and splash clumsily over. I must look like a drunk penguin when I do this.

"Now breaststroke," Madison calls.

I shift back onto my stomach, then spread my arms and start kicking. In . . . out . . . in . . . out . . . in—

I choke from all the water I inhale.

Madison swims over, tutting. "No good. Remember: in, out, in, out."

"I was doing that," I sputter.

"Well, come on. Try again."

"I can't. I have to bike home. Tonight's my parent-teacher conference. Plus I need enough time to shower here so my dad can't tell I've been swimming."

Madison nods. "We'll have tomorrow, at least. But tomorrow's Wednesday, and there's really only Thursday morning to take the test."

"Yeah," I say. Technically the deadline is Friday morning, but Nathan meant Friday morning as in "at breakfast," so there wouldn't be any time to take the test then. And I've still got so many other things to get done too: the vending machine, the kiss, making someone cry, Dad. . . .

"You've made plenty of progress," Madison says as we climb out of the pool. "After tomorrow, you'll be ready."

I look out at the pool, picturing myself trying my hardest in class, in front of people like Ron and Marcellus, and what if I—

If the odds are better than zero, that means there's hope. That means you shouldn't give up on it, no matter what.

I shake the dampness out of my hair. "Yeah. I'll be ready."

Nathan's nowhere to be found when I walk into the house. He's either at Marcellus's or, more likely, he's holed up in his room after his hospital visit. I'm not eager to listen to him gloat about CvC. I'm not eager to listen to him period, really. Mom's not around either. She's got her church thing all night, her one refuge from "her story," the world she thinks is hopeless, the husband she tries to excuse, the kids she can't protect.

I throw some Pop-Tarts in the toaster oven, and right when I finish the last frosted raspberry pastry—those are the best ones, for those keeping score—Dad shows up in the kitchen, ready to go. My cretpoj subject is currently open (no sense giving up after a, uh, false start), and Mom's right about Dad: he really does look like an older version of me, a version of me who's weathered a few storms—

"Something you want to say?"

I lower my head. "No."

The drive to Evergreen is stiffer than a corpse. Dad drives hunched over the steering wheel, eyes constantly scanning for any threats. He doesn't mention Nathan, which means he probably doesn't know. Thank God for small favors. When we make it to school, he parks and leans over to me. "Don't disappoint me."

I gulp.

It's weird being at Evergreen when it's almost dark out. Barely anybody's around. Dad starts walking down the completely wrong hallway. "Dad," I say. "This way."

Dad grumbles. A few seconds later, he makes another wrong turn. "Dad," I call out.

"Bah!" Dad spins on his heel and thunders down the right hall.

When we finally arrive at Miss Richter's room, Dad pulls me aside, right in front of the empty vending machine with Nathan's dirty "For Al" note inside. If he looks to the left a little, would he recognize his son's handwriting? "If I hear one word about any issues . . ."

He doesn't have to finish that sentence.

"You're in the smarter classes. You should use that brain of yours to figure out how to stop making mistakes, goldfish. You've already caused too many problems. Don't do anything else wrong. Understand?"

I nod.

Behind us, Miss Richter clears her throat. Dad inhales like he's been caught shoplifting.

"Hello, Mr. Cole," Miss Richter says. "Hello, Alan. Please come in." She scans my face before she walks into her classroom, Dad and I following behind.

We each take a seat at a desk, forming a little triangle. "I'm happy to be here, Miss Richter," Dad says in the higher-pitched voice he uses when he's not busy being Dad. "It was a delight to meet you two years ago. My oldest son says hi."

"I hope Nathan is well," Miss Richter says. "But let's talk about Alan. I'd like to use the time I have with both of you to talk about Alan's strengths, and how we can both help him along his way."

"Alan has many strengths," Dad says. "Right, Alan?"

"Right," I say without looking up.

Miss Richter points her pencil at Dad. "Can you name one?"

Dad pauses. "What do you mean?"

"I can name many strengths of Alan's, Mr. Cole. Can you name one?"

If I could crumble into the earth, I'd do it right now. Dad looks over at me like this is somehow my fault. We go for forty-three seconds before Dad finally says, "He's . . . a hard worker."

I let out a deep breath. Hard worker? He really thinks that?

"I agree," Miss Richter continues. "He's also creative, conscientious, and good-hearted. Over the past month I've learned that Alan responds best to positive feedback. When he's encouraged, even a little, his confidence skyrockets. I'd like for you to keep that in mind, when you leave here today."

Dad scowls, but doesn't say anything.

Miss Richter pulls a paper from a large pile. "Here's a copy of Alan's recent test scores. . . ."

I practically have to jog to keep up with Dad as he storms out of Miss Richter's room, down the wrong hall. This time I don't correct him, at least not until we've been circling the Sprout science corridor for five minutes. "Dad."

He pivots around to face me, his face like mine, except twisted up in brambles. "What?" he spits.

"I know the way out of here."

"You—" he starts. Then he takes a deep breath. In . . . out . . . in . . . out. "Fine. Go."

With me in front, we navigate the perilous labyrinth that is Evergreen Middle School. Once we finally reach the entrance, Dad exhales.

"Hey, Alan," someone calls. I look up and there's Rudy Brighton, walking with his mom. I wave.

"Man, I heard about your brother," Rudy says. "Looks like he really made a splash, huh?"

All my muscles lock up. "That's great, but we've got to go—"

"He's practically *drowning* in the attention, huh?" Rudy says, grinning.

"Come on, Rudy," Mrs. Brighton says. "We don't want to be late."

"Wait," Dad says. I feel the heat sweeping off him, singeing the grass. "What happened to my son?"

"Oh, you didn't hear?" Rudy asks, completely oblivious. "He was practicing with the swim team, and he tried to dive into the deep end of the pool and wound up almost drowning. The coach had to give him mouth-to-mouth. Boy, I'd hate to be that guy right now. Well, see you later, Alan."

Rudy and his mom walk into the school. Dad isn't moving. "Uh," I say, my voice coming out cracked. "It's almost dark. We should—"

Dad practically sprints to the car.

The car ride is a repeat of our return home from the company dinner, but worse. Dad drives like it's a video game, careening in and out of traffic and screeching around corners and honking when cars completely stop at stop signs. When we get home I'm shaking, but it's not just because of the ride.

Dad slams the door open and yells, "Nathan!" He yells my brother's name three more times, so loud that Mom stands up from the couch, hands clutched to her mouth.

Slowly, Nathan walks downstairs. He shuffles his feet over to me and Dad. "What?" he pouts.

When he sees my brother, Dad's face is completely white. He runs over to Nathan. I brace myself for an explosion, but no—Dad hugs him. He hugs his eldest son, grips him tight, and holds him close.

"Dad!" Nathan gasps. "What the—"

Then Dad lets go. The whiteness flees from a surging tidal wave of red. "What were you *thinking*?" Dad screams, spit flying everywhere. "You idiot! How could you be so stupid?"

"I—what—"

"Diving into the deep end of the pool," Dad yells,

furiously pacing back and forth. "You don't know how to swim. And you joined the swim team? I had no idea your brain was that tiny. How could you possibly be so—so stupid?"

Nathan's mouth falls open. "I—I was—"

"You were *what*? Trying to act cool? Trying to impress your brother? You impressed nobody! I could—I could—"

Ripping himself from his pacing, Dad grabs a nearby lamp and hurls it against the wall, smashing it to pieces.

I duck. Nathan freezes. Mom screams.

Facing away from us, Dad's shoulders heave up and down; his breathing is ragged. Finally, he speaks. "Listen to me and be good. That's all I ask. But you don't. And you almost get yourself . . ." He takes a deep breath. "You should have never been born. All you've ever done, your whole life, is disappoint me. That's all you're good at. Everything you know how to do, you do wrong, except disappoint me. You're a genius at that.

"If I ever—*ever*—catch you near water again—" He turns to Nathan, balls his hands into fists, and storms into the garage.

The heat in the living room is so suffocating I can hardly breathe. I look at my brother, who's white as a sheet, eyes full of raw, rampant fear. Then something cracks, and his face scrunches up, and he runs upstairs before anyone can see his pain.

I look at Mom. Mom looks at me. She disappears into the kitchen, then comes back with a dustpan and broom, sweeping up what's left of the lamp. Her hands shake as she collects the pieces; she keeps glancing at me as she works. Next to the table is a colossal hole in the wall, so big I could stick my hand through.

Once Mom cleans up, she walks upstairs, probably to Nathan's room. I grab the trash bag and take it outside. It's dark out now, and my stomach is growling. I drop the garbage in the bin. As the wind picks up, I stand out there for a while, looking up at the starless, cloudy sky, wondering why I ever thought there was hope at all.

A sudden thud makes me turn around. The window on the top floor overlooking the driveway shuts. That's Nathan's window. On the asphalt—yeah, there's something small there. Slowly I creep over to it.

It's a picture frame. The glass in the frame is cracked, probably from the fall. Inside is a picture of a family: a husband, a wife, and two little boys. The husband has his hand on the wife's knee. The oldest boy is giving a goofy, gap-toothed grin to the camera, while the youngest, no older than four, is laughing on the wife's other knee.

It's the first time I've ever seen the man in the photo

smile like this. A smile of happiness.

Before my grandparents died, this was what we were like.

Suddenly I realize what this is, what this *was*, what it always will be: Nathan's most prized possession.

And he gave it up, tossed it onto the driveway like trash.

I run my finger along the cracked glass, tuck the picture under my arm, and head back inside.

That night I have dreams of rushing water and scorching fire, of a parade of kids with big *loser*s printed on their foreheads, of that horrible sound the lamp made when it crashed against the wall, of Mom's scream. Then I start dreaming of Nathan hovering over my bed, and it isn't until I feel a little chilly that I realize it's not a dream. He's standing over my bed, tearing the covers off.

"Wha . . ." I croak out.

But Nathan's voice comes through crystal clear. "Your phone," he says. "Where is it?"

"My . . . phone?"

"Give me your phone," Nathan says, his voice perfectly even.

Suddenly I'm awake now, rubbing sleep from my eyes.

"Nathan, it's, like, three in the morning. Why do—"

"One more time," he says. "Give me your phone."

Why does he want my phone? Whatever the reason, I'm not doing it. "No," I say. "Take some loose change or something. You can't have my phone."

There's a pause. Then Nathan raises a fist, and smashes it right between my legs.

Everything turns white. I howl out in absolute agony as his knuckles dig in, but he puts a pillow over my face with his other hand so nobody can hear. I've never been in this much pain before. Even when he almost breaks my arm, it's not this bad. I feel like I'm going to barf and cry and explode, oh God, make it stop—

He lifts the pillow up and I'm curled over in the fetal position, sniffling. "Give me your phone," he repeats.

I can barely move, let alone get up to give him my phone. But I don't want another wrecking ball to my private parts, so I moan, "Sock drawer."

Nathan rummages around for a bit, then there's a bright, phone-shaped light shining on his tear-streaked face, then my door slowly shuts, and I'm left behind to pick up the pieces. I don't fall back asleep. I worry about the flames, and whether the fire's going to spread, and what bad things Nathan's planning on doing with my phone. (I also worry about whether I'll ever walk again.

That's kind of important.)

When the sun comes up and my alarm goes off, I'm a mess. Barely slept, hurts to move, gut churning, screaming and crashing sounds in the back of my head. Today can only go up from here.

. . . right?

SEVENTEEN

Wednesday's bus ride, with all its potholes and bumps, isn't too good on my lower body. I try not to wince as I move around, try not to limp as I walk. Trust me: if you're a guy and this has never happened to you, make sure it doesn't, okay?

When I get to the main entrance, there's a crowd around the main bulletin board where all the school clubs post information. Kids are laughing and pointing at something. One of the nice things about that summer growth spurt is I can usually see over most crowds, so it looks like everyone's laughing at—

Oh my God.

Oh God, no.

My legs get wobbly and I almost fall over; I have to

hold on to the wall to keep myself steady. This—this can't be—how did—

He took my phone.

I never deleted the picture after I texted it to Mrs. Truman. I completely forgot about it.

And now it's—it's—

"What's all this?" Madison asks, walking up from the side.

"You should go to homeroom," I whisper.

"What? Why?" Madison asks. "I want to see what everyone's—"

A guy yells, "Hey, there he is!" Soon, the crowd turns its attention on Madison, parting the way toward the photo hanging on the bulletin board, the photo of Madison in a bathing suit, something he never wanted anyone to see.

Madison turns as white as a crumpled-up sheet of paper.

Now I can see the caption, written across the bottom of the photo in handwriting I definitely recognize:

Fatison Truman poses for his glamour shot

Laughter comes from every angle, all directed at Madison. My friend slowly backs up, mouth dangling open, and looks at me with eyes deep with gaping, bleeding hurt. He doesn't have to ask, "How could you?" His eyes do the asking.

I look down.

He starts to sob, and runs away.

The crowd calls after him. "Where you going, Fatison?"

"So he's a crybaby and a fatty, huh?"

"Hey, let's roll him down the stairs like a beach ball!"

"What's going on here?" Principal Dorset yells, walking down the hall. He takes one look at Madison's picture and yanks it off the bulletin board. "Who's responsible for this?" he shouts to the crowd of kids, before all of them run away.

Except me.

"Alan Cole," the principal says. "Do you know who did this?"

I did, I want to say. I gave him my phone. I didn't delete the photo. I was—am—a coward. I could say who did it. I could defend my friend.

I could get punched in the balls again.

"No," I whisper, my head so low I'm practically stooped over.

Madison's not in his seat in homeroom when the bell rings. Maybe he left school early. Maybe he's never coming back. Maybe I was the worst friend in the world, after everything he did for me.

"Hey, where's Fatison?" Rudy asks when Miss Richter shuts the door.

"Shut *up*, Rudy!" Sheila Carter practically screams.

"Yeah, that's not cool," Connor says next to me.

"That's an instant detention, Rudy," Miss Richter says, her voice unyielding. "This classroom is starting a no-tolerance policy for bullying. That applies to anything. One strike and you're out. Are we clear?"

General murmurs. Rudy sinks in his seat a little.

I turn to my left to see what Zack has to say—

—but Zack's not here.

I look at the clock hanging over the door, trying to ignore the beads of sweat forming on my back. He could be running late. Yeah, that's probably it—he took a wrong turn somewhere and stopped to admire a brick with moss. He'll be here any second.

But he isn't here any second. Any minute. We line up to leave.

"Miss Richter," I ask once everyone leaves, "is Zack sick today?"

The teacher shakes her head. "Not that I know of. He was on such a roll with getting here on time too."

I gulp. "Okay. Th-Thanks."

"Alan," Miss Richter says as I walk away. "I hope everything was okay after your parent-teacher conference. You are a good kid. Don't let anyone tell you otherwise, okay?"

I squeeze my eyes shut to stop the tears and leave before she notices.

In swimming I can barely focus. I'm so far behind with CvC; he's up on me by at *least* three, so I really need to pass the test today or tomorrow. But what's the point? There's no way I can beat him. I don't know why I tried, why I thought I had even a tiny chance. I don't know why I thought my art could change the world. I don't know why I thought anything.

Marcellus raises his head at me. "Morning," he says. "Today we're going to—"

"Where's Zack?" I ask.

"Huh?"

"What did he do to Zack?" I whisper.

Marcellus slowly shakes his head. "He does what he wants. I've got no part in it."

"But you know," I plead. "Don't you?"

I look up at Marcellus Mitchell. Quiet, observant Marcellus Mitchell. Is he an introvert, like me? Is it possible we could relate to each other in some way that isn't centered on me being tortured?

"Grab on to the wall," Marcellus says. "Let's see some kicks. Make sure to work real hard when Coach Streit comes over—"

I climb out of the pool.

"What are you doing?" Marcellus asks, a hint of surprise in his voice.

I storm over to the locker room as everyone watches me. "Cole!" Coach Streit calls. "Where are you going?"

I sit down on a bench by my gym locker and shut my eyes. No tears this time. Like Mom.

People like us need to band together. We need to accept our badness and stand up together against everyone else.

"What's your problem?" a voice next to me sneers.

I open my eyes. Oh good. "The coach sent me to check up on you," Ron says. "What's up, nerd? All that screwing around in the water must be getting to you."

"Leave me alone," I whisper.

"Can't do that. Coach Streit wants me to bring your soggy butt back to class. Heard about your brother. You ask me, he makes you look good. At least you're not him."

"I just want to be left alone."

"Fine." Ron shrugs. "Be a little baby. Losers like you make me sick."

"Don't forget 'big' and 'fat,'" I say dully. A happy memory flashes across my brain, but it's quickly drowned in the white noise surrounding everything else. "Big, fat loser. That's me."

Ron shrugs. "Suit yourself."

Once he leaves, I stay in the locker room until everyone else comes in to change. I get a zero in today's class to match the one I'll be getting later in art class. It doesn't matter.

Behind my eyes, flames dance.

It's lonely today at the Unstable Table. Penny gives me the stink eye from behind her scarf as I walk past, and Connor is busy telling a joke at the Stable Table, but there's nobody to sit with me today. Which is good, because I don't deserve any company.

Eventually I hear my name. Connor is waving me over. I ignore him and force some food down my throat.

When I walk into social studies, the first thing I see is Madison, sitting at his desk, looking off to the side. Jenny Cowper snickers when she comes in the room. Everyone else takes a seat, but all our eyes occasionally go to Madison.

"Right," Miss Richter says. "Now—"

There's a knock at the door and one of Principal Dorset's secretaries appears. She motions Miss Richter over and whispers something in her ear. Miss Richter's face twists like she saw three trains crash in the middle of an earthquake, and she addresses the class, "Read pages one twenty-one through one thirty-five. No talking."

Then she's gone.

It takes three seconds for Miss Richter's rule to be broken. "What's that all about?" Rudy asks.

"Somebody probably threw up in the cafeteria again," Shariq says.

"But why would Miss Richter be called away?" Rudy asks. "That doesn't make sense."

Talia adjusts her glasses. "Everyone should be quiet. As your class president, I'll need to report back to Miss Richter if we can't behave."

As the group chats, I look at Madison, head down on his book, buried in his arms. And I know, right then, right there, that I have to make this right, I have to apologize, I have to tell him. I take out my phone (which was on my dresser when I woke up) and type:

my brother took my phone. so so sorry. should have deleted.

Across the room, I hear a little vibration. Madison slowly lifts his head up. He looks down at his phone with red eyes, reads my text, and puts his head back down.

Doesn't even look at me.

That's when I realize he's gone. My friend isn't coming back to me.

I follow Madison's lead and bury my face in my arms.

Miss Richter's gone for half the period. When she comes back, she's clearly not her usual self. She takes a deep breath, then says, "I trust you were all quiet while I was gone."

An electric current of unease runs through everyone. We all look at each other. What could have happened?

When the bell rings, Miss Richter says, "Alan."

The current shocks, jolts. My legs thud along the floor, so slow, so lumbering.

With the room empty, Miss Richter leans forward in her desk. For the first time I see a crack in her armor, a chisel in her steel wall. I notice the name placard on her desk: *Miss Kathleen Richter.* "I want you to tell me the truth," she says. "Do you know what happened to Zack this morning?"

Oh God. Oh no. "No."

"One of the janitors heard humming coming from a locker. Zack was stuffed inside."

I grab on to the wall.

"He refuses to tell us what happened," Miss Richter continues. "They pulled me aside to try to get him to talk about it, but he's keeping quiet. You're friends with him though, so I thought you might know. And you did ask about him this morning. This is a very serious thing that's happened to your friend, Alan. If you know anything about who did this, please tell me."

I can't look up. I can't move. I can't breathe. This is—it's all my—

"Are you . . . ," Miss Richter starts. "You are. You're blaming yourself. Why?"

I croak out, "This wouldn't have happened . . . if Zack . . . and Madison weren't my friends."

"What wouldn't have happened?" Miss Richter asks. "Whatever this is, it isn't your fault."

That's when it finally clicks. That's when it all finally falls into place.

Fire and water and introverts and extroverts and losers and winners and smart kids and being yourself and whether or not people are fundamentally bad. It all sort of . . . *clicks.*

Whatever this is, it isn't your fault.

After eight years of being told it's my fault, I guess I needed someone to say the opposite. To let me realize— maybe it's not.

"Miss Richter," I say, "I am going to make this right."

"You need to tell me what's going on," my teacher says.

"I can't. Not yet. Trust me. I—I think I've got this one."

It's not my fault. I didn't delete the picture and I gave him the phone, but it's not my fault. It's *not my fault.* I didn't do this. This wouldn't have happened if Zack and

Madison weren't my friends, but it could have been any-one I was friendly with. He would have tortured Talia or Connor or Rudy or even Ron if he'd thought they were in my corner.

This is all Nathan Cole's fault.

Sometimes even smart kids need to be taught les-sons. And this goldfish needs to stop being bait for any hyena that goes fishing.

My name is Alan Cole, and I am *not* a coward.

Not anymore.

EIGHTEEN

16 Werther Street looks empty when I get off the bus. Looks. Nathan keeps his bedroom door shut all the time to make sure nobody knows when he's home or at Marcellus's. I walk up the steps anyway, heart thumping a mile a minute, and I knock on the door down the hall from my room.

No answer.

"Open up," I call.

Nothing.

Taking a deep breath, I push the door open.

"Hey!" my brother yells, sitting up from his desk. "Get out of here! Did I say you could come in?"

The walls of Nathan's room are covered with posters for *Star Trek*, *The Lord of the Rings*, and other sci-fi and fantasy movies; his bookshelves are crammed with all kinds of books, from Stephen Hawking to Orson Scott Card to more Tolkien; his desk is full of little wooden toys he built when he was younger, and I know he got so agitated because he doesn't want anyone to know he still plays with them. (Guess what he was doing when I walked in.) "We need to talk," I say.

"Pretty ballsy, young rookie," he says. "But my schedule's full right now. I'll hit you up sometime in the next few days."

"Nathan," I say, trying to fill my voice with as much oomph as I can manage, "I could've gotten you expelled today."

"Greater men than you have tried," Nathan says, waving his hand.

I grunt. "This is serious. I can't believe what you did."

"What I did?" Nathan asks. "Don't you mean what you did? I had to punish you, after all. I've been watching you all week while you goof around with your stupid new friends, even though I was looking for Vic. I learned their names. They weren't Vic. You were the one who gave me your phone, which had all their contact info and an ugly photo of this Fatison jerk in a bathing suit. But he wasn't Vic. You were the one who led this Zack reject on, and all I had to do was send him a text pretending to be you telling him to come to school before any of the buses because I had something important to tell him.

He wasn't Vic either."

My heart aches. Zack was so loyal, he showed up *on time*, and so early. . . .

"I wouldn't have spilled the beans if I found Vic. I was just curious to see what kind of guy my little brother would like. That's all. But I couldn't find him, at school or in your phone or anywhere. I don't know if Vic Valentino even *exists*, you little turd. I think you lied to me. And that made me angry. It's all your fault."

Nathan wanted to punish someone yesterday night, and when he couldn't find Vic's name in my contacts, he settled for Madison and Zack. And me. "No," I say, as firmly as I can. "It's not. It never was. I'm done letting you boss me around."

"Oh yeah?" Nathan asks.

I gulp. "Y-Yeah. I'm done."

"Oh yeah?" Nathan asks.

I don't say anything. My brother cackles his hyena's laugh. "Pathetic. You're ridiculous, Al. You talk so tough, but when was the last time you've ever stood up for yourself? When was the last time you've ever been anything but a total pushover? You're going to be public target number one for the rest of your school career! You didn't forget, did you?"

I squeeze my hands into fists.

"Let's recap the score," Nathan says, ticking items off

his fingers. "Number one: I made you cry. Number two: I found your stupid paper you hid in a stupid spot. Number three: I became the most well-known kid in school, *and* number four: I got my first kiss. Go ahead, try and argue them. I dare you. Last but not least, number five: I gave up my most prized possession. Trust me. So what if I didn't pass the swimming test? So what if I didn't stand up to Dad? I did more than enough. You've only got two."

"Three," I say. "I made someone cry."

Nathan raises his eyebrows. "Who did you—"

"It's not my fault," I say. "But Madison still cried when he saw me act like it was. Most prized possession, well-known, cry. That's three."

"So what?" Nathan asks. "What else are you possibly going to do by the deadline? Stand up to Dad? Like hell you will—you can't even stand up to your own reflection. You'll never be able to get my paper out of the vending machine, because you're a stupid chump. Nobody—girl or guy—will ever want to kiss you. And where would you learn to sw—"

He stops talking, his eyes widening. "So," he growls. "That's what Fatison is doing with you. He's teaching you to swim. You measly little—well, you'll still never do it. You've got one more day to actually pass the test. You can't even take a shower without getting nervous. How are you supposed to swim two lengths of a pool?"

"I'll do it," I say.

Nathan laughs again, finally standing up. I wince. "Where is this coming from? Where do you even get off telling me you'll do anything? You, goldfish extraordinaire? You've never done anything exceptional in your life, and you never will. You're a—"

"Stop it!" I scream.

Both of us stand completely still. Nathan's mouth hangs open, frozen in midsentence.

I recover first. "It doesn't have to be this way," I say, breathing heavy. "We don't have to live like this. We're not—we don't have to be enemies."

"Yes, we do," Nathan says, all the fake friendliness gone from his voice.

"Why?" I plead. "It's not—I'm not *Dad*!"

Nathan recoils, like I've struck him. "You don't get it. That's just like you, to be so oblivious. You've never understood. It's all your fault."

"What is? Nathan, *what* is my fault?"

"You don't even remember!" Nathan growls. "That's the worst part. Before you ruined it, Mom was . . . happy. She smiled real smiles, and hugged me, and after school she would take me to the playground and let me swing on the swings for hours. Even Dad was happier. He came home sometimes with toys for me to play with. He got me my first atlas. He was . . . proud of me."

Nathan jerks his head to the side so I don't see him wiping his eyes on his sleeve.

"But think back: when you got really sick painting that stupid sunset, you got Dad sick too. He screamed at you, then at me when I came home. He kept saying it was your fault, all of it! Mom and Dad, they changed. When was the last time Dad was ever proud of me? Or Mom gave me a real hug? Everything used to be better, until you came along."

I swallow. "That's not the whole story. Our grandparents died that day, and Dad was too sick to visit them. He thinks he could've saved them if I hadn't gotten him sick. Mom told me."

"Oh, she told you, but not me! You've always been the favorite child. Like everyone forgot what you did."

"But I didn't do anything! I never knew the truth until two days ago. Listen to me!"

My brother looks away.

"And Dad doesn't like either of us," I say. "Dad doesn't like anyone! You really think I'm his favorite?"

"Not just Dad's," Nathan says, very quietly.

I shake my head. "You're wrong. You're so wrong. We don't have to fight. Together, me and you can stand up to Dad. We can—"

"You really think so?" Nathan asks, bleeding sarcasm

onto the carpet. "You really think it's sunshine and rainbows, huh? You're even dumber than I thought. You're even dumber than *Dad*, and that's saying a lot."

"Please," I say. "Stop this."

Nathan growls, "Don't tell me what to do." He lunges at me, but I jump out of the way, and he winds up crashing into his desk, scattering all his little toys. He smashes his hands on the desk. "I can't," he says through gritted teeth. "I don't know how. . . ."

"But you do," I say, taking a reluctant step toward him. "You saved my sketchbook. Why do you keep pretending you're someone you're not? Why do you keep pretending you're Dad?"

Nathan turns to me, and there's such a mania, such a fiery frenzy in his eyes, I could melt if I stare at them too long. "Don't you *ever* compare me to him."

Before I can say anything else, Nathan shakes his head back and forth, and when he opens his eyes again they look a little clearer. "This game is to decide the best Cole," he says. "Once and for all."

So that's it. That's why he was freaking out so bad a few days ago when I did those tasks. He's being literal—he really thinks this is the way to see who's the better brother, the better son. The better person. "That's ridiculous," I say. "You need to stop this."

"Stop it?" Nathan laughs. "I'm not stopping it. We're

in this for the long haul. Cole versus Cole, brother versus brother. Winner takes all."

I stand up straight. "Then I'll stop it. I'll stop you. This is the end, Nathan. I—I'll—"

He laughs again, and his laughter follows me out down the hall. I hear it clear as day until he slams his door shut.

When I get to my room and shut my own door, I'm shaking, head to toe. I peer through my blinds at Big Green, oddly still today. I try to control my breathing. In . . . out . . . in . . . out . . . in . . .

I know what I need to do.

I need to get my friends back.

Nathan can't take them from me.

I grab my phone from my pocket and go to type a text, but no. This deserves a (gulp) phone call.

The call goes straight to voice mail. "Hello, this is Madison Wilson Truman. I am unable to get to my phone right now, but if you'd please leave a detailed message after the tone, I will return your call as soon as I am able. I hope you have an outstanding day."

Beep.

Oh God. I didn't—"Madison, it's, uh, it's Alan. Listen, I—I—I'm not going to say I'm sorry again, because, I mean, I should've deleted the picture, but it's my brother, he's the one who took it and put it up, I didn't have anything to do with that, so I guess—"

I take a deep breath.

"You can hate me forever if you want. If you don't want to . . . be my friend ever again, I get it. But I really hope you still do, because I still want to be your friend. Tomorrow I'm going to go out there and try the swimming test, and—and it'd really mean a lot to me if you were in my corner, coach. You and me and Zack, we're friends, and friends stick t-together, and—and—"

I move the phone away from my mouth so the hiccup doesn't come across.

"We can't keep doing this. We can't keep—b-being victims. We need to . . . to stand up for ourselves. You need to come in to school tomorrow, and—and hold your head up, and say, 'My name is M-Madison Wilson Truman, and I'm who I am, and I'm a good, honest, kind person, and nobody can tell me otherwise,' and I'll stand there and be in your corner, like you'd be in mine, because—because we're losers, and losers—"

"Thank you. You have reached the maximum time permitted for recording your message. Good-bye."

A dial tone buzzes in my ear.

I blow my nose, dry my eyes, and hope to God—or whoever feels like paying attention—that he gets the message.

Next up: Zack. But when I look back at my phone,

there's a text already there.

r u goin 2 beat him 2morow

I blink a few times, then text back, very slowly, my thumbs moving one key every three seconds:

better than zero.

NINETEEN

Bus 19 goes a little bit faster Thursday morning to Evergreen Middle School. Maybe it's me, counting down the seconds until show time, but the bus lurches and jostles even more with every pothole than usual. I stare out the window, watching the cars drive by, imagining what my own drawing of a busy suburban street would look like. All the movement and shading and emphasis slips through my fingers, leaks onto the bus floor. I can't paint lying down anymore. It's time to paint standing up.

The doors open. We're here. I walk slowly at first, then I pick up the pace, one foot in front of the other. In . . . out . . . in . . . out . . . I walk by the bulletin board where Madison was humiliated, stopping long enough to see if anyone new is on the chopping block today. In . . . out . . . in . . . out . . . I make it to my locker, peering inside, amazed at how anyone, let alone a twelve-year-old boy, could fit in there for hours . . . in . . . out . . . in . . . out . . .

"Well," a voice behind me says. "I'm surprised you didn't stay home."

Madison has his arms crossed; when he speaks, his voice is softer, higher. "Did you get my message?" I ask.

"You're a bit of a rambler," Madison says. "Are you still planning on taking the test?"

I nod.

"Even though we didn't meet yesterday? You still think you can do it?"

I look down, but nod.

He runs a hand over his hair. "Does it even matter? You still won't beat your brother. He's—"

"Hey, Fatison!" someone yells from down the hall.

Madison shuts his eyes, takes a deep breath, and continues. "He's up on you five to two."

"Five to three," I say. "I made someone cry."

"Who—" He clears his throat. "Well, I'm glad I could help you," he says sarcastically.

"I can do this. I won't let him do this to me anymore. To anyone."

Madison sighs. "Best of luck. I wish I could've been more help."

"Are you kidding? You're my coach. You were amazing."

"Amazing," Madison says bitterly. "A real coach would've gotten you into shape in half the time, and a real coach wouldn't have gotten pictures posted of himself—posted of—"

"Madison, you can't—"

He holds up a hand and walks into homeroom, without me. Shaking my head, I follow.

To my surprise, seated in the desk to my left is Zack, busy looking up at the ceiling. I rush over. "Hi," he says with a broad grin. "You're taking the swimming test today, right?"

"Forget that," I say. "Are you okay?"

"Oh," Zack says. "Yeah, I'm fine. It was kind of fun, actually. I wanted to see how long I could go without making a noise, but then I had to pee, so I started to hum. Lucky for me Mr. Jackson was walking by."

My eyes bug out. "You *wanted* to stay in there without anyone finding you?"

"Sure," Zack says. "New experience, right?"

I look around, making sure Miss Richter isn't watching, and lean closer. "Why didn't you tell them who did it?"

"I couldn't see," Zack says. "I was too busy trying to read the secret code in the ceiling tiles, and they snuck up on me. I didn't think it'd be fair to call out someone I wasn't sure was the culprit."

"But you know who it was."

Zack shrugs. "Probably. But anything's possible."

I try to keep the annoyance from my voice. "I'm glad you're okay."

"Me too," Zack says with a smile. "Hang on a sec." He looks over at Madison, then walks over and says something to him.

"Morning," Connor says from my other side, taking out his gum. "Did I hear that right? Are you taking the swimming test today?"

I turn red. "Oh, uh, maybe."

Connor gives me a big smile. "Good for you, man. I know you can do it."

Still, in spite of everything he said before, those stupid butterflies in my stomach flutter to life when Connor smiles at me. The crumpled-up false-start cretpoj, sitting in the bottom of my backpack, calls my name. I nod. "Th-Thanks."

Before I know it, the bell for first period rings. I freeze in my seat.

"Alan," Zack calls.

I slowly lift myself out of the desk and make my way toward the pool. In . . . out . . . in . . . out . . .

"You can do it," Zack says. "You've got to be confident. You've been practicing every day for, what, a week?"

"Less," I groan.

"Less than a week!" Zack cheers, oblivious. "I know Madison's a good teacher. And you're a good student! You'll do great."

I freeze at the entrance to the locker room.

"Here," Zack says. He holds out my hand and places something small and round in it.

A rock.

I look up. "Zack."

"Just give it back to me when you're done," Zack says. "Keep it in the pocket of your bathing suit."

"It'll fall out."

He shakes his head. "It's never fallen out on me yet. I can't watch you pass the test, but I'll be there in spirit. I want to hear all about it after, okay?"

I hold Zack's most prized possession, the rock that was a gift from his dead father. The rock he's loaning to me. The rock Zack thinks I'm worthy, special, strong enough to hold.

Zack gives me a big hug, right in front of everyone, and he skips off. "Remember the odds," he calls out.

I look at the rock. It's an ordinary-looking stone, round on one side and flat on the other, with gray and tan markings all over. But Zack knows it's not ordinary. And I know it too.

* * *

I change as fast as possible in the locker room, Zack's rock nestled tightly in my right pocket. Before most of the kids come out, I walk up to Coach Streit.

"I hope we won't see a repeat of yesterday, Cole," the coach says. "If that's the case, it is going to be a very long year for you."

"Coach Streit," I say, trying to keep my voice from cracking like it's on a chiropractor's chair, "I'd like to take the swimming test."

The coach squints. "I don't think that's a good idea. Frankly, I've seen your progress in class, and it's lousy. You're not ready."

"Please let me take it. What's the worst that could happen?"

"You sound like your brother. I'm sure you heard what happened to him."

"I'm not like my brother." I muster as much confidence as I can. "I'm me. And I want to take the test. Please."

Coach Streit gives me a long look. She sighs. Once everyone gets changed, she blows her whistle. "Clear out the first lane," she says to the class. "Do warm-ups, but keep the first lane clear." She nods. "You're up. Don't do anything stupid, please."

I climb in from the shallow end. Even though the rest of the class is supposed to be doing warm-ups, they're all watching me. Ron whispers something to the girl next to him, and they both laugh.

"What's this?" Marcellus asks from above me.

"Cole is taking the test," Coach Streit says.

Now the pool is abuzz. "He doesn't know how to swim," Marcellus says.

Coach Streit shrugs. "There's no harm in letting him test his limits. Be ready for when he can't keep going."

Marcellus looks at me very carefully, then stands next to Coach Streit.

I look down the big canal of pool before me, knowing I'll have to swim to the end and come back without stopping. It looks so much longer now, so much vaster and deeper, like Moby-Dick is going to capsize my little speedboat any second.

Everyone's watching me. Everyone's waiting. I can feel the weight of Zack's rock in my pocket. I move my eyes to the locker room, where I could stay and wait and get another zero and not have to worry about this—

—and there's Madison, standing by the doors, watching.

We look at each other for a bit. Slowly, very slowly, he raises his fist and gives me a thumbs-up.

Like a bullet, I kick off from the wall.

One arm over the other, turning my head sideways as I swim freestyle down the pool. I flutter kick, making huge splashes as I plod along, careful not to stop for anything. My hair gets soggy and flops around, but I can see just fine, and before I know it, I'm at the deep end.

I can hear people squawking and yelling and even a few cheers as I flop onto my back, drunken penguin style, and paddle my way halfway across the pool. The ceiling lights look so bright, so intense, shining down on me. My arms and legs ache from (less than) a week's practice, but I keep pushing, and Coach Streit blows her whistle when I reach the halfway point, which I know is the cue to start the breaststroke.

Now for the real test.

I pause to orient myself: arms pointed out, legs in the back. I propel myself forward, but it's no good, and I get a mouth full of pool water. I choke a little. I can hear the screams of my classmates louder, I can hear Coach Streit yelling encouragement, I can hear—

Then I stop, because at the end of the pool, at the shallow end where I started, is the goal. The end result. The finish line.

Like a superhero fighting an epic battle against a giant monster, I push out with my arms, slapping the water, waves crashing all around me, cascading into mini tsunamis. I am a titan. I am a juggernaut. I am powerful, tough, strong. I did this. I became this way through hard work and training and I am not a victim anymore.

No more.

The outside world—all those people, all those lights, all those sounds and distractions and judgments—fades away, and all I see is the goal.

I look up.

I keep looking up until I'm at the end, and I climb out of the pool, and I almost fall over as Madison tackles me to the ground, laughing and screaming, and all the noise rushes back in and the pool is a tidal wave of energy directed at me.

I did it.

Coach Streit blows her whistle a bunch, but nobody is listening, and soon I'm lifted to my feet, given claps on the back and hands through my hair and fist bumps and for this moment, I am king.

I did it.

I really, really did it.

Madison is beside himself, pumping his fists into the air, fully dressed and dripping wet and hollering like a lunatic. I look at my friend, and he looks at me, and we grin and laugh. Everything is as good as—better than—it's ever been.

Of course, Madison winds up getting a detention for cutting class, but he doesn't care. "I knew you could do it," he says one last time as Coach Streit makes him leave. "I always believed in you. Even when things got—

even when we—I always believed . . ."

Once all the excitement wears off, Marcellus walks over to me. "Kid," he says, "where'd you learn to swim like that?"

I look up. "I had a good teacher."

If I didn't know better, I'd swear Marcellus almost cracks a smile. "All right," he says.

Even Ron's impressed. Well, I assume Ron's impressed, because he doesn't say anything mean to me. He just sneers in the locker room. I'll take it.

When I catch up with Zack later, he practically runs me over with a bear hug steamroller. I give him back his rock. "Thanks," I say. "I think it helped."

Zack shakes his head. "That was all you."

And in the end, as word spreads throughout Evergreen one more time about Mr. Where-Do-Babies-Come-From, I didn't do it for CvC. I didn't do it to impress Nathan or to make Madison happy. I did it because I wanted to do it. Because, after twelve years of looking down, I wanted to look up at the world for once, to see the world head-on, to not be afraid. That's the real test I took today, and I passed it with flying colors.

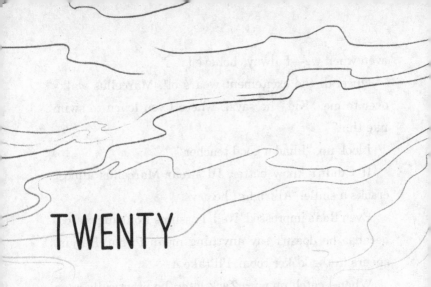

TWENTY

It's right before lunch, right after art, and I'm at my locker getting my books ready for the second half of the day, when my open locker door slams shut, nearly crushing my fingers.

"What," Nathan says, speaking very precisely, "do you think you're doing?"

I look up. "I'm stopping you. Once and for all. If I need to win CvC to do it, then that's what I'll do."

"You?" Nathan spits, taking his hand from my locker. "You can't stop me. You think you're so smart—you think you're so tough—I'll *destroy* you, goldfish."

"Nathan," a voice behind my brother says.

Marcellus places a hand on Nathan's shoulder, but Nathan shrugs him off. "Don't you start," Nathan growls. "You had one job, Marcellus! You needed to make sure

Boy Blunder here didn't learn to swim! And he did! He *learned*! He—"

"Leave the kid alone," Marcellus says evenly. "He worked hard. Let him have it."

"Let him—are you out of your mind?" Nathan whirls around, facing his only friend. "Whose side are you on? You probably helped him learn behind my back, just—just because!"

Marcellus's stoic face shifts. Kids in the hall slow down and stop as Nathan gets louder and more agitated.

"Alan, what's going on?" Madison asks, coming up the hall with Zack. Madison stops when he sees Nathan.

"Hi," Zack says. "You must be Alan's brother. It's nice to meet you. From the front, I guess."

Nathan growls again. "You're stupid. You're all stupid. Stupid Al with his stupid friends and his stupid swimming and his stupid *everything*. I won't lose to you, you little—" Nathan suddenly stops, seemingly aware of all the people watching him.

Madison draws himself up to his full height. "Nathan Cole, I don't care what petty, jealous thugs like you think of me. Do your worst." He crosses his arms and stares right into my brother's eyes.

"Petty," Nathan whispers. "Jealous?" He looks around the hall, calculating, number crunching.

"If I were you, Nathan," Miss Richter says, coming

out of her room, holding her tote bag, extendable pointer poking out of the top, "I'd walk away. Fast."

The crowd whispers, the crowd points, the crowd watches. I take a step toward my brother. "It's over," I say.

Nathan's voice trembles a little. "Not yet. Good luck reaching into that stupid vending machine to get your stupid paper, or getting a stupid kiss, you stupid—"

"What did I just say?" Miss Richter says, setting down her bag. "Move it along, and leave my students alone."

Good luck reaching into that stupid vending machine.

It can't be. It can't . . . is it . . . really that easy?

No, of course not. He had to put something on the tip to make it stick, and that's why the paper is so dirty, to hide the *actual* stain. He planned it all out to confuse me. Well, I'm not confused anymore.

Miss Richter tells Nathan to get lost or he's getting a detention, and Nathan stammers something about me, and Marcellus keeps putting his hand on Nathan's shoulder, and most of the crowd still hovers around because they smell blood in the air, and Madison and Zack flank me like they're bodyguards, and Mrs. Ront tries to take all these kids clogging up the hall and scatter them to the winds, and as for me? I dash over to Miss Richter's bag and grab her extendable pointer stick while she's busy with Nathan. Then I look into the crowd and sure enough, there's Connor, poking his head up behind a Shrub's shoulders to watch whatever's going to happen.

I run up to him. "Need your gum."

"Huh?" he asks.

"No time to explain. Just—can you spit out your gum? And give it to me?"

Connor gives me a weird look, and Ron yells, "Come on, fight that other kid already! I got five bucks on you going down in ten seconds," and next thing I know Connor's handing me a used gum wrapper.

"Whatever you're doing," Connor says over the noise, "you better hurry. Your brother looks mad."

Sure enough, Nathan is still being chewed out by Miss Richter, but he looks like he's ready to bark back at her any second. He's still not paying attention to me—matter of fact, everyone's focused on watching my brother get lectured by a teacher, everyone except Zack and Madison. "What are you doing?" Madison asks me as I walk a few feet down the hall. "Are you running aw—"

Zack watches me stick Connor's chewed-up gum to the tip of the pointer stick, and grins. Madison, too, figures it out as I approach the vending machine. "Wow," he murmurs.

After a good bit of maneuvering, I wiggle the pointer stick inside the machine. I hit the button to make it extend—come on—almost there—

"Hey, everybody," Ron yells. "Cole's trying to break into that vending machine."

Now the crowd's attention snaps back to me. "Stop!" Nathan cries. "Stop it! Don't do that!"

My arm starts to cramp up from the angle—almost got it that time—come on—come on come on come on—

"Stop!" Nathan yells, dashing down the hall, darting through other kids. "Stop stop stop stop stooooooop!"

Then, with a faint crinkling noise, the gum latches onto the paper. I pull everything out of the machine, a great smile across my face.

"Yeah!" Zack pumps his fist, and Madison gasps, and someone yells, "Whoa!" and someone else yells, "Ew!" and there's clapping and cheering. Nathan's now three feet from me. His knees get weak; his shoulders sag. He looks down. I peel the paper off the gum and hand it to him.

The crowd is mostly silent, but there's a low hum in the air, a crackle, like when lightning's about to strike in a still lake.

Stuck behind two Shrubs, Talia attempts to step forward. "I hope you're all happy now. That paper is gone, so now there's no reason to keep the machine around. As Sapling class president, it will be—"

Low chuckling cuts Talia off. "Is that it?" my brother

growl-whispers, standing up straight again. "Is that all you've got?"

Against the wall, Miss Richter nods to a third teacher, who takes off down the hall, toward Principal Dorset's office.

"That's it," Nathan says. He looks up, and in his eyes there's rage and flame like I've never seen before. "I'm telling."

My stomach flips over. "*What?*"

"I'm telling," Nathan says. "I'm tired of keeping my promises. What good's it ever done me? I just want to destroy you, you stupid goldfish. It's all your fault. So I'll do it. I'll tell them. I'll tell them all. Then won't you be sorry you thought you were smarter than me?" He holds the last word out, screeches it, lets it linger.

"You can't—you've never—you said—you *can't*—"

"Oh yeah?" my brother says. "Watch me."

I freeze.

He grins a devil's grin, licking his lips. "May the best Cole win."

Sometimes, some things need to be done. Sometimes they're not obvious, sometimes they're not pleasant. Right now, in the hallway of Evergreen Middle School, with an entire army of kids watching, it's not the most obvious thing to do. It's one of the most terrifying things to do.

It needs to be done. I guess usually what you *need* to do isn't always the same as what you *want* to do. But now I know what I need to do.

Maybe, deep down, I want to do it too.

I look back at Zack, clearly on the same wavelength, and he gives me a thumbs-up.

So I take a step away from Nathan, into the crowd, toward one kid standing against the wall.

"What's going on?" Connor asks.

In . . . out . . . in . . . out . . . in . . . ignore everyone watching me . . . ignore my gut tumbling around . . . in . . . out . . . in . . . "I have to tell you something."

"Uh, okay," Connor says. "Can it wait until lunch? I mean, it's cool you got that thing out of the machine and all, but you can keep the gum—"

"Itsgottobenow," I say as one big word. In . . . out . . . in—out—in—out—"Connor—I—"

"Okay," Miss Richter calls over the crowd. "Anyone still here in fifteen seconds is getting a detenti—"

"I like you."

A hush falls over the crowd.

Connor blinks. "Huh?"

I don't look down. "I've . . . always liked you. You don't have to like me back or—or anything, but I—I just wanted you to know."

Connor's mouth drops.

Slowly, I turn around. Nathan looks like a car that's slammed into a telephone pole, but worse. All the fire's gone from his eyes, from his heart. Now it's empty. *He's* empty. He watches me, then eventually pushes past the crowd and walks away. Marcellus hesitates, then follows him.

I feel all tingly. I'm trembling. I have tears in my eyes. And I'm smiling. Smiling the biggest smile I've ever smiled, like that little boy in Nathan's photo. Like a dam bursting open, I realize then and there who my cretpoj—the real one—is going to be. And I can't *wait* to start it.

First things first, of course. The ripple spreads almost immediately, and soon everyone in the crowd knows. Several kids laugh, chief among them Ron, who blurts out, "You're kidding me, right? What a little—"

"What did I say about getting to class?" Miss Richter says, and like her words are a knife through a thick cake, the crowd finally parts. Connor watches me, mouth still open. Once all the kids scatter, he wanders off with Ron like he's in a daze.

Zack throws an arm around my shoulder as we walk toward the cafeteria. "You did it!" he cries. "How do you feel?"

"Nervous," I say. "Scared. But . . . I think I'm happy too." I look at Madison. "Sorry for not telling you."

Madison's arms are folded over his chest. "I understand why you didn't. Of course, if Connor doesn't make a good boyfriend, I can put my matchmaking skills to the test."

"You?" I ask.

"Of course!" Madison puffs out his chest as we navigate the crowd. "I'm a master of the human psyche."

"Okay," Zack says. "What am I thinking right now?"

Madison shakes his head and smiles. "Normal human psyche. Not Zack human psyche."

"Wrong!" Zack says. "I was thinking how much fun it'd be to be a ballpoint pen."

I laugh. "I've got to hear this."

"Well," Zack says, "pens are full of ink, like octopuses, and everyone loves octopuses, so can you imagine carrying around a little mini octopus in your pocket . . ."

TWENTY-ONE

A wide gap follows us, like the parting of the Red Sea, as we walk through the cafeteria to get in line. Nobody wants to get close to me. They might catch "the gay disease," or maybe something even worse. Contamination. It's a fog I have to cut through as we get our food.

But I cut through it.

The Unstable Table shimmies as we sit down. I eat my salty Tater Tots, ignoring all the stares. "Hey," Zack says, "what's the difference between an ostrich and a sanding belt?"

"What?" I ask.

"An ostrich has an *o* in its name," Zack says. "Boy, English is confusing. F w ddn't hv vwls t wld b vn wrs. That's No-Vowel for—"

Something thwacks me on the back of my ear. I cup

a hand to my head to stop the stinging and look behind me to see Ron, laughing at the Stable Table, readying another perfect shot with another pencil.

"Ignore them," Madison says. "They're not worth it."

I don't look at Ron, or at almost all the other people at his table. I look at the one kid there who isn't laughing. Connor sits quietly, gazing at the wall.

"What do you think he's thinking about?" Zack asks.

"I don't know."

Another pencil. This one hits my shoulder.

A teacher comes over and tells Ron to knock it off, which makes the pencils stop, but it doesn't stop him from sticking *that* finger in the air (you know the one) and dangling it around, low enough so the teachers won't see but high enough for me to notice.

Connor still doesn't move.

Why do we get crushes on people? It's so random. Zack had it bad for Penny even though she was kind of a psychopath, and I've got it bad for Connor even though he's kind of a homophobe. What's even the deal?

"Alan Cole," a bossy voice says. "You've really gotten yourself into a mess of trouble this time, haven't you?"

Madison wrinkles his nose. "If you've come to make fun of Alan, you can take it up with me first."

Talia pushes up her glasses. "I'm Sapling class president. I represent all students equally, regardless of race, gender, or sexual orientation. This is why *I'm* class president and *you're* not."

Madison opens his mouth again, but I cut him off and ask, "What is it, Talia?"

"I came by to tell you the student council supports you and all your life choices. That's all. It's obvious I'm not wanted here, so I'll go now." She pauses. "Good luck."

"Wait," I say before she walks away. I look back at Ron and his friends, currently going "Aaaaaalaaaan, Aaaaaalaaaan" over and over again under their breath. "Are you still looking for an idea to make a difference in school?"

Talia perks up. "Of course I am."

"And you still want to pay me back for the election?"

She nods. "Use my favor or lose it."

I motion for Madison, Zack, and Talia to huddle around me, and I smile. "Let me tell you about my cretpoj."

When I get home, Mom is doing dishes in the kitchen. She looks at the clock on the wall, the clock that's absorbed years, maybe generations of memories. It ticks, tocks, ticks, tocks. In, out, in, out.

I walk up to Mom and give her a hug.

At first she doesn't react. Then, slowly but surely, her arms wrap around my back, and we embrace. When

I break free, her face looks different, like she almost remembers what muscles you need to work to make you hug a person. The last time we hugged, she was taller than me.

Then I see someone sitting at the kitchen table. Nathan is spacing out, playing with one of his toys, a little top he whittled when he was five with his name painted on every inch. He keeps spinning it, watching it fall over, spinning it, watching it fall over, spinning it.

I watch my brother. Mom watches him too. He doesn't even acknowledge we're there. His eyes are glazed over, foggy. He's checked out.

My focus snaps away from Nathan as the front door slams shut.

Mom's whole body tightens.

Dad walks in and smashes his briefcase onto the kitchen table, knocking Nathan's top over. He massages his temples and looks around the kitchen, taking in Mom, then me, then finally Nathan. With one swift movement he extends his talons and snatches up Nathan's top. Nathan, still in a daze, barely reacts. Dad hands it to me. The message is clear: get rid of this.

I take the top, admiring the little, shaky *Nathan*s across it. I wonder what five-year-old Nathan felt when he wrote this. Pride at being able to spell his name when he was so young? Desire to put his name out there, wherever he could, however he could?

Dad is watching me, fiery eyes shooting heat vision. Mom is watching me too, hands over her mouth. I look up at Dad, walk to the kitchen table, and give the top back to Nathan.

My brother finally blinks, finally notices I'm there. He looks at me, then Dad. Me, Dad. Me, Dad.

My father grabs the top from the table again. This time he doesn't give it to me. Instead, he walks over to the garbage can and drops the top inside.

Nathan watches, dull eyes taking in the scene. He looks down.

I walk over to the trash can and pick up the top. I brush off the little bit of lettuce on the tip, then I hand it back to Nathan, laying it right next to his hand. His eyes bug out. He looks at me, then Dad. Me, Dad.

Dad lets out a low, guttural growl. I raise my eyes to him, unblinking. We stare at each other, father and son, mirror images separated by age.

He raises a fist and winds it up behind him.

"Jimmy!"

He stops in midpunch.

Mom calls out again, "Jimmy!"

Dad looks at her, at Cindy Cole, his wife, the mother of his two children. He looks at me as I shake but still stand, like he hasn't looked at me in forever. He looks at Nathan the same way. He looks at his fist, now also shaking.

He lowers his fist.

His breathing comes loud and hard, his shoulders heaving with an irregular beat. His eyes aren't the eyes of a hawk. They're the eyes of a man. A very, very scared man.

He takes a very sharp breath. Then another. Like the oceans are opening under him. Like he's fighting a rising flood. Like he's out to sea as a great tidal wave strikes.

Like he's drowning.

Moving one foot in front of the other, Dad leaves the kitchen and walks upstairs.

Mom puts her hands over her heart. After looking at me and Nathan, she follows her husband upstairs.

Then it's just Nathan and me in the kitchen.

I walk over to the table and pick up the top. Gently I push the toy into Nathan's hands. I close his fingers around it.

We watch each other. Cole and Cole.

I head upstairs.

It's a quiet night at 16 Werther Street. Only Mom and I sit at the table for dinner. She takes a plate up to Dad and Nathan, but otherwise the table is missing half the family. Mom and I talk a little, mostly about the food. At the end of the meal, she smiles at me. An honest, genuine smile.

That night, after dinner, I grab my new sketchbook, and I start my cretpoj.

TWENTY-TWO

The mid-October sun peeks through the clouds when I wake up Friday morning. Big Green dances through my blinds, and if I search hard enough I can see the traces of red and yellow and orange on the tips of the leaves. My sketchbook sits on my desk, its first page now taken up with the outline of the most awe-inspiring, gravity-defying, throat-screeching cretpoj known to man.

"Alan!" Mom calls from downstairs.

Shoot. I'll miss the bus if I don't hurry. I head down to the breakfast table, and sitting there with a cup of coffee is Dad. The morning paper lies by him, unread. He sips his coffee and stares off into space.

When I'm done inhaling my bowl of Lucky Charms, Mom motions me over and gives me a kiss on the cheek. It makes me feel . . . fuller. Warmer. Stronger. Like there's a mini sun inside my chest. A simple cross, the one she wore to the company dinner, hangs around her neck. She smiles again as I head out the door.

"Alan."

Dad's voice stops me.

Without looking up, Dad says, "Today, do your best."

My breath catches in my throat. I don't reply.

Dad picks up his paper and takes another sip of coffee. Maybe he doesn't realize this is the first time he's ever actually wished me well in anything.

But maybe he does.

Maybe I'm not the only one learning to swim.

I walk outside, my steps almost in rhythm with the wooden clock, into the sun.

At Evergreen, there's still an Alan quarantine going on. Most kids don't want to get near me or even look at me, which you'd think might make me happy. Don't get me wrong: introverts like me can always use a little more peace and quiet, but I wish it didn't come with a price.

Oh well. I'd rather have a hard time being myself than an easy time being somebody else. Wise words, those.

When I get to homeroom, I hear, "Hey." Surprise, surprise, it's Ron, walking toward me with a menacing sneer. "What's up, homo? Been dreaming about my friend lately?"

I look up at Ron. "I don't have to answer that."

Ron laughs really loudly, making people stop and stare. "Oh, you don't, huh? If I ever see you talk to Connor again, or try to turn him into a gay little piece of crap like you, I'll—"

"He can talk to me if he wants," Connor says, walking up behind me.

I turn bright red.

Ron looks like he stepped in something and it's slowly seeping up his pants leg. "What are you talking about? Why would you—"

"Because Alan's cool," Connor says. "So lay off him, okay? You know I'll cream you in a fight, so don't even act like you're some tough guy. Leave him alone. All right?"

Ron scowls. He raises both hands and walks into his homeroom.

I look at Connor. He's not smiling. "I—I—" I stammer.

"I don't like you," Connor says. "Okay? I'm not into . . . that. I like girls."

"Okay," I say slowly.

He continues, "But I don't care what you like to do or who you crush on—though I guess I'd be happier if it wasn't, y'know, me." Now he smiles a little.

I don't return his smile. "It's not my fault."

Connor sighs. "I guess it's not. I'm sorry for being a jerk. I shouldn't have called Ron gay the other day. But you know we can't ever, like, uh, date and stuff, right? Cause I like girls, and you're, y'know, not a girl?"

"I know," I say, still finding this whole conversation a little surreal. "I guess I'll get over you eventually."

Connor makes a fist like he's going to playfully punch me on the arm, but he stops shy of my sleeve, and he walks into homeroom without saying anything else. I let the heat from his hand wash over me and I shiver a little, and the tightness in my chest expands.

In homeroom, Miss Richter takes roll. Talia isn't in her seat. From across the room and in the seat next to me, Madison and Zack both give me thumbs-ups. I return with a whopping thumb of my own.

Principal Dorset comes on the loudspeaker for the morning announcements. After the usual boring junk, he says, "I would like to introduce Sapling Class President Talia MacDonald, who proposed a new initiative to me yesterday. Talia?"

"Thank you, Principal Dorset," Talia says. Her voice is clear and confident, I guess because she can't see any of her audience this time. "One of my goals as class president was to bring competitive drive back to Evergreen. The more I thought about it, however, the more I realized maybe we were already competing too much. Maybe we need to be cooperating more instead."

Me, Zack, and Madison all grin.

Talia continues, "In tribute to my class president debate, I've titled this project 'Where Do We Come From?'"

(That was Zack's idea. Madison also thought it'd be a good way to get people more sympathetic to the idea.)

"Every student at Evergreen shares a diverse experience," Talia says. "Whether it's race or gender, body shape or hair color, family status or sexual orientation—"

(everyone in homeroom looks at me)

"—we're all different. But we also forget we're similar too. Kids have been teased and bullied for such small things, when we all share the same story. One thing I've learned is sometimes it takes a portrait of someone's life to really understand who they are. It's my hope that 'Where Do We Come From?' will be a great way to talk about our differences in a way that encourages discussion and openness. Anyone can contribute art, essays, videos, and many more outlets for display in the hall. We're all different, but we're also all similar. I hope this project helps people realize that. Thank you very much."

Miss Richter claps loudly, and even though most of the people in the room don't join in, Madison yells, "Hear, hear," and Zack gives a standing ovation and whistles. In the other seat next to me, Connor looks over at me for a bit and eventually gives me a big smile. I give one right back.

After all, I'm not the only person in the world who can make a cretpoj.

At the end of homeroom, Miss Richter calls me over. I rummage around in my bag for her extendable pointer, which I didn't want to give back to her right away yesterday, but she shakes her head. "You keep it," she says. "A little souvenir. Besides, I'm not sure I'd want to use it anymore after it got all gummed up."

"Thanks," I say.

"I heard you passed the swimming test."

I nod.

"Well, good job. I'm proud of you, but I hope more than anything you're proud of yourself."

"I am."

Miss Richter looks at me and smiles. "You look happier today. Like you threw up a giant slug that was infesting your belly."

I make a face. "Gross."

"I try," Miss Richter says. "The rest of seventh grade beckons. What's next for Alan Cole?"

What's next? "I'd like to finish learning the periodic table, I guess. Maybe study more verbs—"

"That isn't what I mean."

"I know. Can I get back to you?"

She smiles. "It's okay to not know. What matters is that you keep looking. Never stop looking."

I smile too. "Thanks." I pause. "For everything."

Miss Richter sips her coffee.

As I leave homeroom, I realize the business with Ron made me forget to get stuff out of my locker, so I walk over there. That's when I see him. In the midst of loud crowds and empty vending machines, he walks toward me, head down, hands in his pockets. I let him approach.

"You won," Nathan says.

"Huh?"

We're almost the same height, Nathan and me. He looks me in the eyes. "You won. Six to five. The game's over. Tell me what you want me to do."

Oh my God. I guess I did win, but . . . "Nathan, you don't have to—"

"Just tell me what favor you want me to do. That's your prize for winning. I always keep my promises. Especially after . . . after last night." His voice wavers. "Go ahead. Say whatever you want. I'll do it."

I haven't thought about this at all. Even when I pulled ahead in points yesterday, I never gave it any thought. How can I ask anything of Nathan? How can I—

No. There is something. "Okay."

He winces, awaiting his judgment. His punishment.

"My favor I'm asking," I say, "is for you to not become like Dad."

"What?"

"You said the favor can't involve anything that would harm you. So here it is. Don't ever become like Dad. Use your smarts for good. Don't let darkness take you over. Even if Dad changes, don't be like how he was. That's my wish."

"I can't do that," Nathan says, trembling, looking down again.

"You have to," I say. "You always keep your promises, right?"

Nathan squeezes his hands into fists.

"Nathan," I say, "you can do it."

My brother raises his head, takes a deep breath, and opens his eyes. "You're really something else, you know that?" he asks me. "You little punk."

I don't move.

He extends his hand. "Just keep me in line if I lose it."

The lava inside my gut evaporates. Not all of it, but a lot of it, so much that I break into a wide, cheek-to-cheek grin. I shake Nathan's hand. "You've got a deal."

Nathan nods. "Maybe you're not such a bad guy after all, Alan."

* * *

"—so the moose says to the cow, 'Hey buddy, get off my lawn!'" Zack chuckles, pounding his fist on the Unstable Table. "Hoo boy, that was a good one."

"I've been thinking," Madison says after he swallows a big bite of kale. "My next project. Now that Alan is up to snuff in swimming class."

"Are you going to teach people how to balance a checkbook?" Zack asks. "Mine always falls off the tightrope."

Madison blinks. "Now that I've proven I can do something on my own, I can focus on self-improvement."

"Like losing fifteen pounds by the end of the month?" Zack asks.

Madison makes a sour face. "I'll need to discuss that with my parents."

A kid walks by the Unstable Table and says, "Hey, Fatison."

Madison crosses his arms. "What's your name?"

The kid stops walking. "Uh, George."

"My name is Madison Wilson Truman. I took the trouble to learn your name, George, so the least you could do is learn mine."

The kid hovers awkwardly around our table for a bit, then leaves.

Zack grins. "That was awesome."

I smile. "Yeah. And you don't have to take me to Helen's Crest anymore, so you won't have any excuse to be there."

"Actually," Madison says, "if you want my honest opinion, I'd like you to go with me, so I *do* have an excuse. That way it won't be quite so bad."

"Sure," I say. "That sounds fun. Maybe we can do something else instead of swimming."

"Hey, there's Penny," Zack yells. "Hi, Penny!"

From a few tables down, Penny moves her head in a motion that perfectly syncs up with an eye roll.

"She doesn't know what she's missing," I say.

Zack nods. "It's okay. There'll be other girls. And other guys." He gives me a wink.

I glance over at the Stable Table, thinking about the one CvC task I didn't complete.

"Even losers don't have to lose all the time," Zack says. "Whatever happens down the road—good and bad—we'll face it together."

"Yes," Madison says. "You don't have to worry about that, Alan."

I smile. "I'm not worried. I'm not worried at all."

The noise of the cafeteria, all the chatter and the clutter, all of it fades away as Madison, Zack, and I place our thumbs in the center of the Unstable Table. We're losers. But we'll never lose what really counts.

* * *

At my desk in my bedroom there sits a little mirror. Next to the mirror is my sketchbook, with paints and pencils aligned in rows. Inside the mirror there's a face, a face with long black hair and bright eyes. No shadowy fire in that face. No dark flames scorching the edges.

I brush the hair out of my eyes and capture myself inside my cretpoj, a goldfish becoming a man.

ACKNOWLEDGMENTS

Thank you to Joy McCullough-Carranza, my mentor in the 2015 Pitch Wars contest, for your keen editorial eye, for nurturing me at all levels of development, and for believing no question I asked was too small or too stupid. Thank you to Pitch Wars mentors Rebecca Wells, Jessica Vitalis, and Brooks Benjamin for feedback, support, and confidence boosts. Thank you to Brenda Drake and her team of dedicated mentors for making dreams possible.

Thank you to Brent Taylor, my agent, for endless encouragement, unwavering faith, and our shared commitment to the message behind the book—you believe in Alan just as much as I do. Thank you to Uwe Stender for being a huge advocate for me and my work.

Thank you to Ben Rosenthal, my editor at Katherine Tegen Books, for excellent editorial feedback and for welcoming my input at all levels. Thank you to Julia Kuo for a brilliant and evocative cover. Thank you to Mabel Hsu and the rest of the staff at HarperCollins for all your tireless work on the book and for inviting me to peer behind the mystical curtain of publishing. Thank you to Katherine Tegen for trusting in Alan and trusting in me.

Thank you to the Bux-Mont Critique Group—Wendy Greenley, Tamara C. Gureghian, Jean Ladden, Joanne Alburger, Debbie Dadey, and Melissa McDaniel—for helping shape the manuscript from its earliest stages with honest critiquing and warm encouragement.

Thank you to Rachel Kobin for helping me get on my feet, both professionally and personally, and for inspiring me to reclaim my authorial voice. Thank you to my friends and fellow writers at the Philadelphia Writers Workshop for helping me grow in my journey as a writer. Thank you to Michael Lynch for inspiring the title of this book.

Thank you to the Barn Raisers—Connie Morby, Kristen Strocchia, Lilace Guignard, and Marcia Gregorio—for insightful feedback and for helping the earliest versions of Alan, Zack, and Madison take shape.

Thank you to my beta readers and trusted writing buddies: Stephen Kittel, Parag S. Gohel, Louis R. Artfich, Eric Jenkins, and Solim and Glenn Chung.

Thank you to my trusted sources of inspiration who helped me with ideas: David Labe, Alan Huan Chang, Brett Finnicum, Andreana Lau, Rafael A. Mora Moreu, Jessica Choi, Margie Hammett, Richie George, Summer Heacock, and Jennifer Norman.

And thank you for inviting me—and Alan—into your world. My world is a little bit brighter every time someone reads my book, and I can only hope yours brightens every time you read it too.

Turn the page for a sneak peek at
Alan Cole Doesn't Dance

ONE

A wise philosopher once said, "Personal change is like a slow, painful, heaving round of vomit. It's gross and embarrassing while it happens, but relieving and kind of refreshing when you're done." I think it's an ancient proverb.

Whether there's metaphorical puke or not—in my case I've spent more time blowing long hair out of my eyes than blowing chunks over a toilet—I realize now that the hardest thing about personal change is how the person you leave behind and the person you're on your way to becoming don't fully line up at first, like a shaky hand on paper. But that shaky hand gets steady eventually, and before you know it you're used to the new change. And that's that.

Except, of course, you're never done changing.

"Hey, Alan," Zack interrupts my inner monologue with a chipper whisper. "Do you think the radioactive man-beasts come out of that little tube?"

I squint at the Mercury Nuclear Power Plant's pressurized water reactor (at least that's what the tour guide called it). "I don't think they'd fit," I whisper back.

"Radioactive man-beasts can stretch and contort their bodies into all kinds of shapes," Zack says. "I bet if we asked Francine really nicely, she'd tell us the truth."

I don't think Francine, our tour guide, wants to answer Zack's questions, let alone cart around a bunch of middle schoolers on a field trip. When Miss Richter said all the Accelerated School Placement Enrichment and Nourishment (ASPEN) classes, seventh graders through ninth graders (so that's Saplings, Sprouts, and Shrubs, in ascending order—yep, you read that right), were taking a field trip to a nuclear plant, I thought it'd be more exciting than watching water rush around. Zack keeps insisting Francine is "hiding the deadly truths about nuclear power" due to government conspiracies.

"Hush," Madison whispers, putting a finger to his mouth. "You're missing all the important facts."

"Who can tell me the difference between nuclear fission and nuclear fusion?" Francine asks.

Madison's hand shoots into the air. "Nuclear fission

involves the splitting of atoms, whereas nuclear fusion involves the joining of atoms," he recites.

"That's right," Francine says.

"Fatison could use some splitting of his atoms, huh?" an eighth-grade (I try not to use the plant terminology if I can help it, because I have some measure of self-respect) girl whispers, leading to some nearby snickering.

"Hmph." Madison crosses his arms but doesn't say anything in response.

As we move away from the pressurized water reactor, I say to Madison, "I bet they're jealous. They probably didn't know what nuclear fission was before—"

Someone bumps into me, hard from behind, knocking me off balance. Zack reaches out to steady me. "Hey!" he yelps.

"Oh sorry," a ninth-grade guy says. "Didn't see you there, Galan."

The guy walks away without a teacher noticing. Madison sighs. "At least *Fatison* is on its way out. I worry there's a lot more mileage they'll be getting from *Galan*."

"The name doesn't even make sense," Zack says. "It sounds like a prescription drug."

"Gay Alan," Madison mutters.

Zack's eyes get wide. "Ohhhhh. I get it now. Wouldn't it be *Gaylan* then? You should petition to change the

3

name. If they're going to make fun of you, they should at least *try*. Right?"

My reputation as the guy who likes other guys came about a month ago, at the end of my brother Nathan's game of Cole vs. Cole, or CvC. Nathan, who'd practically made a full-time job out of turning my life into a waking nightmare, threatened to out me to all of Evergreen Middle School if I lost the game. And even though I won, I still came out because I wanted to stop being afraid of my brother, and of the rest of the world. Now I'm getting to know a loud minority of kids who think it's funny to call me *Galan*, who like to taunt and shove me when the teachers aren't looking. It's like I've traded in one gigantic bully for a bunch of smaller ones.

Right now my attention is focused on Nathan, two years my senior, hovering within earshot. He watches me, I guess to make sure I'm not hurt, even though he could've intervened but didn't. Marcellus Mitchell, his best friend, whispers something in his ear, and Nathan makes this jerky half-step in my direction, but then he and Marcellus leave us behind.

"It's been a month," Zack says as we catch up with the rest of the group. "I'm surprised he hasn't stood up for you."

"Not once," I say.

"Hmph," Madison scoffs. "If you want my honest

opinion, I'm not surprised. He tortured you for years. Someone with such a cruel streak isn't going to change on a dime." He frowns. "Or ever."

After I won CvC, I made Nathan swear off his dark ways. I guess I didn't specify he had to actively be a good person though. He's barely said one word to me this past month, which is, granted, a huge improvement over the past twelve years of our relationship. But I was hoping for a normal big brother. One who sticks up for his little bro if his little bro runs into homophobia every day.

The giant clump of kids congregates around what looks like a gift shop. "We're offering a special twenty-five-percent student discount on Mercury Power Plant merchandise," Francine says like she's reading off a tele-prompter.

"Do you have T-shirts?" Rudy Brighton, my seventh-grade classmate, asks.

"We've got a few," Francine says.

Rudy pumps his fist into the air and leads the way into the gift shop.

Instead of walking into the incredibly fascinating gift shop, Miss Richter, my favorite teacher, snaps her fingers. "None of that," she says to someone I can't see. I crane my neck and—

Ugh.

Connor Garcia—the straight guy I'm still, despite

knowing it'll never work out between us, crushing on—is laughing, flashing his big smile at Sheila Carter. She gets to see a lot of his big smile lately because Connor and Sheila are officially a *couple*. Officially *dating*. Officially getting into plenty of PDA *every single day*, which is totally gross and I'm not jealous at all. Nope. Why would you get that idea?

I force my eye to stop twitching.

"Alan Cole," a voice from behind me barks, startling me so much my skeleton practically jumps out of my skin.

"Hi," I say in between deep breaths.

Talia MacDonald, our class president, doesn't look happy. Then again, Talia hasn't looked happy much lately. Maybe the stress of running an entire grade is getting to her. She's pitched three million ideas to Principal Dorset for "ways to improve the middle school experience," and he's only approved one of them. And I know that one idea is why she wants to talk to me.

"You know why I want to talk to you," she says. (What did I tell you?)

I nod. "Because there's too many people to fit into the gift shop."

Talia puts her hands on her hips. "This isn't a laughing matter. I tried to launch 'Where Do We Come From?' a month ago, and I've only had three participants. I keep waiting for an Alan Cole masterpiece to christen the display, but thus far you've given me absolutely squat."

She's right. And it burns. Last month I shared with Talia (and Zack and Madison) the idea for my cretpoj, the painting that became my self-portrait. That inspired Talia's big project about understanding each other. That's what I want to do with my cretpoj: change the world. It would make sense for me to contribute something that shows where I came from. Who I am. What I believe in. But . . .

"It's not done," I say. "I'll let you know when it is."

"You keep saying that," Talia says, shaking her head. "I'm starting to think you don't want anyone to see your . . . crunkpot, was it?"

"Cretpoj."

"Whatever it is, I want it. If I have to grab that sketchbook of yours and squeeze it out with my bare hands, I will. Don't test me!" She stomps off toward the crowded gift shop.

I breathe easier. My hands pat my sketchbook reflexively, nestled in my backpack. The truth is . . . my cretpoj is done. It's been done for three weeks. I spent hours cooped up in my room with a tiny mirror and my paints, making the most whiplashing, neck-cracking, earthquake-inducing, pressurized-water-reacting painting known to humanity. It's going to make the whole world throw up.

I have shown it to absolutely no one.

I love to paint. I live to paint. If art was breathing, I'd cry watercolors. Zack and Madison keep asking me about it. Talia keeps asking me about it. The world is waiting for me to unveil it. Why can't I even take it out of my sketchbook?

When I think about my cretpoj just sitting in my sketchbook turning yellow, it makes me sick. To make things even worse, I haven't painted anything at all since I finished it. No people, no puppies, no plants. Not even stick figures. For all the good I've done over the past month, it all starts to unravel whenever I think about the fact that I'm sitting on my purpose in life, hands firmly squashed under my butt, losing muscle memory, turning to dust. What's the problem? What am I afraid of?

"You okay?" Zack asks as the classes awkwardly shovel themselves into the gift shop. He's already changed into an "I <3 My Power Plant" T-shirt.

"I'm fine," I say. If I keep telling myself that, I will be.

Madison puffs out his chest. He clutches a mug with a nuclear reactor design that says "The Fission Commission." "Well, gentlemen, I'd say this field trip was a fantastic success. We learned so much about nuclear power and how safe and efficient it is."

"We didn't learn about the radioactive man-beasts

though," Zack says. "Do you think this shirt brings out the color in my hair?"

"You don't need any help drawing attention to your hair," Madison says.

Zack picks at a loose strand of his bird's nest of a hairstyle, flopping in between his eyebrows. "I guess not. Hey, slumber party this weekend?"

I perk up. "That'd be great."

"For the last time, call them *sleepovers*," Madison groans. "Much more mature. I'll need to check with my parents, but it should be fine."

Zack smiles. "Best friends. Now and forever."

We all bump fists, extending and touching our thumbs.

I'll let you in on a little secret—sometimes I think I haven't changed enough yet. Sometimes I look at my friends, so brave and strong, and I see in myself something else. Sometimes I look at my cretpoj, and I don't see the Alan of tomorrow. I see the Alan of yesterday, a yesterday I hoped I'd left behind. That's the thing about change: it's hard—but hopefully it's doable too. So I keep changing. I keep struggling. And maybe eventually, maybe someday, my shaky hands will make a masterpiece.

DATE DUE

FOLLETT